# The Twisted Shadow

# THE TWISTED SHADOW

by **Edith Dorian**

JD7337

*Whittlesey House*

McGRAW-HILL BOOK COMPANY, INC.

NEW YORK   TORONTO   LONDON

*Published by Whittlesey House
A Division of the McGraw-Hill Book Company, Inc.
Printed in the United States of America*

*For Timothy Wallace Brown of Rutgers University*
*whose roommates at last count included:*

*1 chicken snake*
*6 pine snakes*
*1 king snake*
*3 ribbon snakes*
*1 brown water snake*
*1 yellow-bellied water snake*
*1 coachwhip snake*
*1 southern banded snake*
*1 boa constrictor*
*6 chameleons*
*4 skinks*
*1 squirrel tree frog*
*1 narrow-mouthed toad*
*3 green tree toads*
*2 box turtles*
*1 gopher tortoise*
*2 Anderson tree frogs*
*1 marble salamander*
*1 alligator*
*1 scorpion*
           *and*
*3 Sigma Phi Epsilon fraternity brothers*

# Contents

## 1 · *Don't Tread on Me!*

JUDY Carrington drove the station wagon through the entrance into Gun Point National Park and patted the steering wheel triumphantly. Not even a leaf of the lilac hedge had brushed her fender.

"Just the same," she told the station wagon, "if you weren't so new and snooty-looking, I wouldn't be afraid I'd get gray hair worrying about you."

Thinking back, she only hoped she had looked a lot less surprised than she felt when she first saw the Sinnett Harbor Library after her train had pulled in from New York yesterday afternoon. Because her mental picture of a library in a small Maine town had definitely not included either a colonial-style brick building with a handsome new wing almost ready for use or a bookmobile like this one.

A big, sprawling log cabin marked "Ranger Station" stood to the left of the road, and Judy glanced at it curiously. She had three books illustrated with pic-

9

tures of unappetizing reptiles for somebody in that building. Besides, unless she wanted to find the cabins on her route by the eeny-meeny-miney-mo system, she needed a Park map. She might have been brought up on stories of Sinnett Harbor, but she had been there exactly twenty-four hours, and Gun Point National Park was new since her mother's day anyway. In fact, as far as Judy could see, her mother would never recognize her home town.

Thirty years ago, before Grandfather Mariner died and Grandmother moved her family to Massachusetts, Sinnett Harbor had been a quiet fishing port, not a summer resort for writers and publishers. Now there was not much along Ship Street any of the Mariners would remember except the First Parish Church on the ancient Mall, and even that was flanked by new buildings like the post office, the town hall, and the library.

Shadows were capering over the shiny new paint of the station wagon, and Judy watched their antics with amusement as she hunted out the books for the Ranger Station. One of those shadows was fantastically appropriate. No matter how often it dissolved and reformed, it managed to resemble a gallows. Conditioned imagination, she decided, chuckling. That's what came of driving on Gallows Road. By the time she'd done it regularly, twice a week for two months, she'd be likely to think she saw some luckless pirate, sitting on his coffin, jolting in a cart to execution on Gibbet Ridge!

Sliding the doors over the bookshelves again, she

looked idly over her shoulder to see what was causing her macabre shadow. Then she nearly dropped the ranger's reptiles in astonishment. Either termites did not eat gibbets or the town fathers had set up a replica of the original model to give tourists their money's worth. Fascinated, Judy examined the plaque attached to its upright. It was the Sinnett Harbor gallows all right; at least, it was the last one ever used, thriftily moved to serve as a signpost to Gibbet Ridge. At least that eliminated one of the three forks in the road for her bookmobile route. She already knew who lived on the Ridge nowadays—Sinnett Harbor's most famous native son, the Pulitzer Prize winner, Sandys Winter. She ought to know; she had written a term paper on his novels for her Contemporary American Literature course this spring.

Judy shook her head as she hurried across the road to the log cabin. She was beginning to feel sorry for the rangers. A life-sized gallows was not exactly a soul-satisfying summer view. She preferred her own of Pound o' Tea Lighthouse and the open bay beyond the harbor breakwaters. But her sympathy for rangers was short-lived. Nobody answered her repeated bangs with the knocker, and she finally tramped back to the bookmobile minus the Park map she wanted.

"What's the good of a ranger station without a ranger?" she muttered. "If those men think I'm leaving library books on a front porch that practically sits on a public road, they're in for a shock."

Disgustedly she dumped the books on the seat beside

11

her and started off again. She supposed she could stop at the Station on the way back. Meanwhile, she might as well try the right-hand fork. It was closer.

That fork, however, seemed to be a total loss for a cabin hunter. It was not much more than a trail at best, and Judy began to wonder what road etiquette demanded if another car appeared from the opposite direction. Probably one of them backed all the way to its starting point to let the other through. But after she had stopped for the fourth time to give a white-tailed deer the right of way, she would have been less surprised to meet a war party of Penobscots padding along in moccasins than anything as blatantly civilized as another car. If there were people and cabins in the woods on either side of this narrow dirt track, those deer were mighty unconcerned about them. It was a pair of skunks, though, waddling placidly out of the bushes almost into the path of the bookmobile, that made Judy try another direction. Slamming on her brakes, she spotted a winding side road and hastily turned into that. She was not arguing with one skunk, let alone two. That fork had been getting her nowhere fast. If they wanted it, they could have it.

Nevertheless, before she had gone more than a quarter of a mile, she was thinking of those skunks with positive affection. From the sounds ahead of her, she must be nearly on top of a dozen families with five small boys apiece! But a boy chasing a ball was no more predictable than a skunk, and she crawled around the last curve at a safety-first ten miles an hour. This time she had no need to worry, however. There were plenty of boys—a whole pack of cub scouts on a camporee apparently— but they were much too busy building a fireplace on the beach to get under her wheels. She even had to honk a couple of times before they noticed the bookmobile and came swarming back over the meadow.

"We're the first contingent," the cubmaster explained. "There'll be cubs and scouts alternating in these cabins every two weeks till Labor Day." He grinned at Judy cheerfully. "I thought maybe you'd like a warning since we'll want books for badge work, everything from crafts to outdoor cooking. One thing's sure; we'll all scrape the bottom of your barrel for wildlife material. This summer one of the rangers is taking the boys on regularly."

Judy smiled at him. "Thanks for the warning," she said. "We'll manage all right at the library unless you descend like a plague of locusts. I've got some of the things you want aboard the bookmobile now, and next time I'll come loaded."

The next half hour was lively enough to leave Judy breathless, and even after she had drafted two high-school-age den chiefs to list what was going off the shelves, she still felt as if she were managing a three-ring circus.

"On Friday I'll be here earlier," she promised, "and stay a whole hour. Then each den can come up in turn with its own den chief and have fifteen minutes to find books. The den that wins cabin inspection oftenest gets to come first. Okay?"

13

Their shout of approval made her laugh. Cubs might be strenuous, but they were fun. This was one stop in the Park she was going to enjoy. Most of them had never seen a bookmobile before, and they crowded close to watch her shut up shop.

"Where are you going next?" they demanded. "Over to Breakfast Cove?" Judy pricked up her ears. These kids sounded as if they knew their way around.

"I wouldn't know," she told them sadly, "not unless you help me. This bookmobile hasn't got a compass, and I've been lost for hours."

After that, instructions came so fast she had to beg for mercy. The boys had been exploring the Park since early morning, and if there was a single cabin they had not located, it was invisible.

"Draw me a map. You can put X's in for cabins instead of treasure," she suggested, and one of the boys dropped down to set to work in the dirt with a stick.

He was the young imp with the angelic smile and mischief in his eyes who had been disappointed because she did not have any snake books on the shelves, and Judy wrestled with temptation while she copied his map. In her opinion, it would be no more than poetic justice if she handed him one of those reptile books on the front seat as a reward for doing some ranger's job for him. Only she knew perfectly well they were too technical, and she climbed into the station wagon with her conscience still free.

"I'll bring you *two* snake books for sure next time,"

14

she called as she drove off, and his face lighted up happily.

She thought of the youngster again when she finally finished her cabin rounds and headed back to the Ranger Station for her last stop. If one of the rangers was boning up on snakes, that kid would get a terrific bang out of talking to him, and she ought to do something about it. She did not have much idea of what rangers were like; probably they were pretty rough and rugged. Just the same, it couldn't hurt to tackle him.

Judy had got herself all steamed up over her idea long before she reached the Station, but her enthusiasm did not do her much good. Nobody answered her knock this time either. She hated to cart their books back to the library until Friday. On the other hand, she had no more intention of leaving them on that front porch than she had had earlier. For a minute she hesitated, undecided. Then she made up her mind and walked briskly around to the back of the building, looking for a less conspicuous spot.

Luck was with her. There was another door in an ell made by a rear shed, and she stacked the books on its doorstep with a sigh of relief. She was through. She would find the ranger for her cub, though, when she came back at the end of the week. He could not elude her forever.

From a pine branch almost over her head a squirrel started to scold angrily, and Judy looked up to laugh at him.

15

"What's the matter with you?" she asked. "I don't want your nuts."

The squirrel jerked his tail convulsively and danced with rage.

"All right, I'm really Daniel Boone," she admitted, "but you're safe anyway. I'm in too much of a hurry to shoot you for a stew."

Still watching his antics, she hopped off the step only to stop and listen again. Now something was hissing like a basketball with a bad leak. Puzzled, she glanced down at the path and recoiled in horror. Stretched out in front of her was the largest snake she had ever seen. Then while she stood there, frozen, persistently and unmistakably his tail began to rattle.

With a curious objective detachment, Judy could hear her own voice rising in a scream. But screaming wouldn't help, she thought wildly. That was what the squirrel was doing and he was safe in a tree. Desperately she jumped back on the doorstep and grabbed for a book. If she could make that thing strike at something, she might get past him.

Her hands icy, she scaled the book at the snake's head and got ready to run. Only suddenly there was no need. A human rocket in a green uniform was already diving across the path.

"Hey, quit it!" he shouted indignantly. "You'll hurt that snake!"

## 2 · *Assistant Ranger Timothy Wade*

THE color flamed back into Judy's face as she gaped down at the top of the ranger's dark head. She had never been more furious at anyone in her life.

"What do you mean don't hurt him?" she snapped. "He was rattling his tail. I heard him."

"Of course he was," the ranger said. He struggled to his feet with two yards of snake in his arms, and eyed her reproachfully. "Wouldn't you make fierce noises if somebody tried to tramp on you?"

His voice sounded so aggrieved that Judy felt herself beginning to laugh. Then, to her dismay, she discovered she couldn't stop. The more alarmed the ranger looked, the harder she laughed.

"Here, stop that," he ordered, and Judy promptly stopped to glare at him. Who did he think he was to order her around? He couldn't be more than a year or so older than she was! She opened her mouth to say something withering, but he didn't give her a chance.

"Relax, will you?" he begged. "Nobody's found a poisonous snake in Maine for a hundred years. This pine snake was just putting on a show so you'd leave him alone. If you'd come look at his eyes, you'd know next time. Rattlers have elliptical pupils. This snake's are round as marbles."

But Judy refused to budge.

"I don't care *what* he is," she said firmly. "I still don't like him."

"Well, you would if you knew him better," the ranger assured her. "Believe it or not, snakes make good pets." He scratched the pine snake under the chin and smiled at her cheerfully. "This fellow's a summer resident like you. I drove him down from New Jersey."

Fortunately for her blood pressure, Judy was too aghast even to notice the comparison. She was staring at him, appalled.

"You mean you actually had that thing in a car with you?" she demanded. "What were you trying to do, panic the parkways?"

"Okay, okay, you win," the ranger conceded soothingly. "If you don't like him, you don't like him." Looking resigned, he hooked a stout, screened cage out from under a bayberry bush with his foot and deposited the snake inside.

Judy, however, still registered a marked lack of enthusiasm for the whole situation. A little whittled stick stuck through a hasp failed to impress her as an adequate way to secure a six-foot reptile mean enough to imitate a rattlesnake. But the ranger straightened up

18

again acting as if everything were now under control.

"Maybe I'd better introduce myself," he said. "Assistant Ranger Timothy Wade, at your service. Do you want a key to a cabin or are you just looking for friends?"

"Neither," Judy retorted with dignity. "I'm Judith Carrington from the bookmobile." Retrieving the book she had thrown at the snake, she added the two from the doorstep and handed them over in a neat stack. "These must be yours," she said frostily. "But we don't have the book on Brazilian antivenoms yet. We had to order it." Then turning on her heel, she was about to start for the station wagon when she thought of something else. "And if it comes, *you* can walk out to the bookmobile to get it. Hereafter, I only stop and honk."

Get stuck on a date with that ranger and you'd need a mongoose, Judy thought crossly as she headed the bookmobile up Gallows Road. It was a miracle he didn't hiss when he talked! Maybe she should have stayed where she belonged and worked in the New York Public Library again. But after all, she ought to be able to ignore one ranger; the rest of them were probably human. And she did not like humid heat. New York was perfect for college in the winter; it just was not her idea of a summer resort. That was why she had jumped at this job when the Personnel Bureau at Barnard had told her about it, she reminded herself—that and the fact that Sinnett Harbor made her family seem nearer. Even after all these years, her mother still had a Harbor accent. Her father must be right; a born State of Mainer was always a State of Mainer. He claimed you could scratch the surface of any of them, no matter how long they had been away, and come spang up against a Maine ledge every time.

Judy shelved the obnoxious ranger, and put her mind firmly back on the road. On her bookmobile route map, Sinnett Harbor looked like a big mitten dropped down on Pentecost Bay, and Gallows Road ran between the tall pines of the Park preserve and the salt water of the Bay's inlet right along the edge of its gargantuan thumb. What kept surprising Judy about it was the lack of traffic. Somehow, with the entrance to the National Park at the end, she had expected campers to be hiking all over the scenery. Instead it ribboned emptily out ahead of her. She had not seen another car all afternoon. Except for its paving, Gallows Road must look exactly as it had in her mother's childhood. For that matter, it probably had not even changed since the eighteenth century when the notorious pirate, Bold Dick, used to anchor his *Sea Hawk* impudently off Gibbet Ridge practically in the shadow of the town gallows!

Remembering Bold Dick set Judy's thoughts wandering again. Ever since she had written that term paper in American lit., she had been wondering why Sandys Winter had waited till last year to write *Rogue's Hour*. She would have thought Bold Dick was a natural for one of his first books. After all, not every novelist had a handy piratical ancestor who struck his Jolly Roger and came sailing home to haul his ship's eighteen-pounders onto Gun Point in the nick of time to save his native town from the British. Mr. Winter even still lived in the same house Bold Dick had built after he rescued his lovely Tory, Charity Royalle, from the gallows to marry her. At least, though, when Mr. Winter did get around to writing *Rogue's Hour,* it had won him the Pulitzer Prize for the second time, and the movie version had just captured Oscars for half its cast.

For a barefoot boy from a salt-water farm who had sailed on a fishing schooner to earn money to go to college, Sandys Winter had certainly acquired the Midas touch, Judy decided. Everything he wrote turned into a smash-hit movie. It was strange that he had never married. His pictures looked distinguished enough, definitely Park Avenue tailoring and Dunhill pipes. Maybe success had turned him into a stuffed shirt. Anyway, she was likely to find out soon. She had not been in the library an hour this morning before she discovered he was the member of the board of trustees who had given the new wing.

A pair of Great Blue Herons flapped down in the marsh grass along the inlet and Judy promptly forgot everything else. She even stopped the station wagon a while to watch them, and when she got going again, she no longer had Gallows Road to herself. A Model A was chugging toward her from town, but it seemed to be pulling over to the shoulder. Maybe her herons had lighted farther on now. When she looked at the Ford the next time, however, the driver was bending over its hood.

Of all the deserted places to get stuck in, Judy thought sympathetically as she stopped alongside the white-haired man in hip boots and salt-stained dungarees who was struggling with a crank. "Couldn't I give you a push, or a lift or something?" she asked.

"A push would do it," the man said gratefully. "She seems set against being cranked." He smiled at Judy, his deep-set eyes startlingly blue in his weathered face. "I stopped to plug a lobster claw and my starter went dead."

Judy nodded cheerfully. "Okay, here we go," she said, and maneuvered until she could drive in behind him.

"I don't dare stop again, but I'm much obliged," he called out his window as his car got going once more. "We'll meet soon anyway."

Listening to the familiar chug-chug, Judy chuckled to herself. She thought it highly probable. With an obstinate starter and an ornery crank, he was likely to be still stuck near a Park cabin on her Friday trip if he had to stop to deliver his lobsters. So far this had been quite a day!

The rest of it was peaceful enough, however, and she spent the evening placidly unpacking and writing a ten-page letter to her family. Consequently, it was irritating to have snakes on her mind again before she could even get down to breakfast the next morning. Her brand-new lipstick had turned up missing, and she knew she had had it in her pocket right up to the minute she encountered that ranger's repulsive reptile. Judy was in no humor to be philosophical about it either, not with payday four days off. Screwing up the two lipsticks she had on her bureau, she eyed them both with a grimace of distaste. If she had to make out with those stubs until Friday afternoon, somebody was bound to think she was trying to land a clown's job with Ringling Brothers, Barnum and Bailey. Worst of all, "somebody" was likely to be her landlord and landlady, Captain and Mrs. Matthew Dunning—and Captain Matt was chairman of the library board.

As a matter of fact, however, the effect Judy achieved with one of those stubs was unlike any clown's mouth on record, and Captain Matt's shrewd blue eyes twinkled as he watched her swing up the harbor's Foreside past his workshop after breakfast.

"Blonde and jet-propelled," he remarked to his wife with interest, and Jen Dunning smiled at him.

"I shouldn't wonder if the breeze around the library blew a mite brisker than it's blown for quite a spell," she agreed cheerfully.

But that Tuesday morning the breeze around the library was already brisk enough to suit Judy. She had her hands full with something called "Bold Dick Week." Sinnett Harbor, she had learned, was about to celebrate the 175th anniversary of its famous escape from the British during the Revolution, and though it was possible someone in the town might not be on a committee, nothing happened to make Judy think it was probable. The library bulged all day with committee members hunting for weird information—like the ingredients of whipped sillabub or the proper way to fasten a hangman's noose.

About five-thirty, though, when she dashed out to the

nearest drugstore to grab a sandwich and a cup of coffee for supper, Judy began to look confidently forward to an evening lull. With weather like this, nobody in his right mind was going to coop himself up if he could stay outside and watch a full moon rise over Pentecost Bay. But she had failed to reckon with Sinnett Harbor's Yankee thoroughness. By six-thirty two committees had already put Miss Leonard, the head librarian, and her senior assistant, Miss Addison, out of action, and by seven Judy was wishing she were twins. Barry St. Leger, the director of the summer theater, had marched in with a slew of costume and scenery people in his wake, and she was doing a marathon between the circulation desk and the table they had preempted.

Being asked to help find books on period costumes she took in her stride, but a casual request for the original Hollywood sketches of the *Rogue's Hour* costumes made her eyes pop. She would never have suspected that the Sinnett Harbor Library owned them and she had no idea where to start looking. Then when she did locate them, Sandys Winter's longhand manuscript of *Rogue's Hour* was stowed away in the same file drawer! And to top that, the men who had asked for the costume sketches turned out to be Broadway's famous Sam Runner and Joe Harne, in town because they had done a musical version of the Winter book for Bold Dick Week. *The Lady and the Pirate* they told her it was called.

Back on her perch behind the circulation desk for a few minutes, Judy grinned to herself. She was suddenly imagining her college roommate's face if she

24

walked in and discovered Broadway in the reference room. According to Babs, working in a library was the equivalent of sealing yourself in a tomb, and she thought Judy was crazy to plan to go to library school.

"Why spend your life among fossils while the world wags by?" she argued. "Me for an office. I want to see something that at least looks like a date once in a while!"

Judy glanced at the playwrights across the room and grinned again. Mr. Runner and Mr. Harne might not qualify as dates, but Babs would certainly never classify them among the fossils. With her passion for the theater, she'd be standing on her ear in excitement.

Eventually even the theater people drifted out the door, though, and Judy promptly tackled the job of getting reference books back on the shelves. It was already twenty minutes of nine and she was not aching to stay overtime. The thought of Miss Leonard and Miss Addison stuck in the new wing with their committees troubled her, however. Obviously she could not walk out and leave them holding the bag. They must be dead on their feet. Still, twenty minutes were twenty minutes. They might all get out of the building on time yet. At least no one else would come in now.

Actually Judy cherished that comforting idea for less than seven minutes. The door latch clicked again, and she spun around to start back to the circulation desk, trying to look like a welcome mat and a time clock simultaneously. But she dropped the welcome part of the act in a hurry. Thirteen minutes to closing and she had to cope with Assistant Ranger Timothy Wade!

## 3 · Lipstick and Lobster Rolls

J UDY looked pointedly from Ranger Wade to the clock. "This library closes at nine sharp," she informed him. "You'll have to hurry if you want a book. Snakes are classified under 598—over there in the stacks at the back of the room."

Her tone was as warm and cordial as an icicle, but Ranger Wade chose to ignore it.

"Thanks," he said blandly. "I'll have a look." He held out his palm with a cylinder of lipstick on it. "I thought I'd better stop by with this. You dropped it at the Station yesterday."

Judy hastily thawed several degrees. "Oh swell, thanks," she said happily. "I've been moaning over it all day." Just the same she still had no intention of letting him keep her overtime. There was no sense in encouraging people to stroll in at the last minute or nobody'd ever get out of the place. "Don't forget you have only seven minutes," she said over her shoulder as she headed back to her books. "Please call if you need help."

But when Miss Leonard hurried across the room five minutes later, Judy had finished her replacement job uninterrupted.

"Time to close shop," the librarian said. "Just leave a light on the desk and put the latch on the door as you go, please, will you, Judy?"

"What about you and Miss Addison?" Judy asked. "It won't kill me to stay if you need me, you know."

But Miss Leonard shook her head. "Miss Addison's already shooed one committee out the back door and escaped," she told Judy, smiling. "The other may be around for another half hour, but I'm a member of it anyway so that's my funeral. You trot along."

Then, hearing footsteps in the stacks, she raised her eyebrows. "Some one still here?" she asked in surprise.

"One of the rangers," Judy said.

"Well, don't let him hold you up," Miss Leonard advised her, and Judy laughed.

"Don't worry, he won't," she said cheerfully as she settled behind the desk with both eyes glued on the clock, and Miss Leonard vanished, chuckling.

One minute to go. Half a minute. Nine! Judy banged three card drawers shut in rapid succession. That ought to do it, she thought with satisfaction.

It did. Ranger Wade dutifully reappeared with a book clutched in his hand and strode over to the desk.

"Anything in the regulations against my taking out another?" he asked. "You brought me three yesterday."

"Nothing at all," Judy said briskly, "the quota's four. If you'll just sign the cards, I'll check it right out."

But when he handed her the *Nature Guide to Reptiles and Amphibians,* she was annoyed again. Only this time it was herself she wanted to kick. She had meant to stick that away in the bookmobile at lunch hour for her snake-minded cub.

"Isn't this a little elementary for you?" she asked in her best professional tone. "I was thinking of taking it over to a cub scout in the Park."

"To the towhead with the grin?" the ranger asked. "He's the one I'm getting it for. He's working on a reptile badge."

"Oh," Judy said, and did another mental about-face. If she'd had any brains, she'd have known yesterday. This was a man she had to work with all summer! "Then if you're the ranger who's taking those kids on for nature badges, you'd better show me what books you want me to bring over there. Besides, I promised that towhead two snake books. Just wait till I find a pad and you can come pick them out for me."

She rummaged hastily in the top desk drawer, and Ranger Wade looked up at the clock. "My ears are going back on me," he announced. "I thought you said I had to be out at nine o'clock sharp!"

"Under normal circumstances," Judy said calmly as she steered him toward the stacks. "But these aren't normal. Once you get back in Junior's clutches, you'll probably never show up again. I'm surprised he let you out tonight."

"Junior?" the ranger repeated, puzzled. "Junior who?"

"The slithering serpent," Judy explained. "That pine snake or whatever you called him. How is he, by the way?"

"Doing as well as could be expected considering the scare you gave him," Ranger Wade retorted, and Judy hoisted storm signals again.

The ranger, however, refused to be intimidated. "Look," he said plaintively, "why don't you declare a truce? I practically never carry serpents coiled around my middle. We could even go fifty-fifty: I forgive you for picking on Junior and me, and you forgive us for existing. Then we could go eat lobster rolls in peace and practice first names. After all, we have to work together."

He sounded so absurd that Judy laughed in spite of herself. Maybe he wasn't so bad. At least he had a sense of humor.

He grinned back at her cheerfully. "Here's your pencil," he said. "Come on and get this over with. I should never have mentioned those lobster rolls. I can feel myself starving."

But he was still alive a half hour later when they settled on a couple of stools at the Whistling Clam with their sandwich rolls and coffee.

"I'm glad you made me stop and pick that stuff out," he admitted. "It'll make working with those kids all summer a whole lot easier. Your library's okay on its wildlife collection, Judy."

"It's pretty much okay anyway as far as I can tell from just two days," Judy said. "Miss Leonard seems to buy books as if the budget grew in the United States mint. That library rocked me right back on my heels when I first saw it. You see, my mother was born and brought up here, and I guess I thought the town was still the same—just a few hundred year-rounders, not even any summer people."

"Well, you weren't any greener than I was," Tim consoled her. "The national parks I'd met were out in the country with maybe a general store and a movie in a nearby village. I nearly flipped when I saw Ship Street."

"That's one thing I still don't get," Judy said frankly, "why you're here, I mean. Back at the library you didn't make Maine sound like good snake country."

"But you've got to admit it's swell summer country," he pointed out, "and who's a wildlife-management major to snoot any national-park job in vacation? Right now I only think I'm a herpetologist. I start graduate work this fall."

"Then you're one up on me," Judy told him. "I've got another year at Barnard before I start library school. I didn't know about summer rangers, though. I figured you were 'ranging' around here permanently."

"No reason not to," he agreed. "Plenty of wildlife-management majors go in for ranger work—only I'd be down in the Everglades where you don't need a magnifying glass to find a snake!"

"Why not South America?" she asked. "Brazil

maybe. Isn't that supposed to be tops for snakes?"

"Got a plane ticket in your pocket?" he demanded, and Judy made a wry face.

"If I had, I'd use it myself," she informed him. "My family's down there and I haven't seen them for two years! Dad's in the consular service."

But she shook her head vigorously at his barrage of questions. "There's no use asking me about the place. Jaunting to Porto Alegre and back vacations is hard on the pocketbook. I've stayed in the States. Anyway, this summer Dad and Mother were supposed to come home for a couple of months. Now they won't be back till fall."

"The least you could do is adopt me," Tim said, "but do you offer? No! And I'd make a lovely foster child."

"I'm panting for the opportunity," Judy assured him. "I can't imagine anything sweeter than you and a couple of bushmasters romping around a kitchen." She wagged her head regretfully, however. "Only I don't recommend it. In the consular service you never can tell. Just when everything was legal, zoom, Dad'd be transferred, and considering St. Patrick, wouldn't you look cute in Ireland!"

"Perish the thought," Tim said with horror. "Let's get out of here before you think of anything worse."

The full moon was riding high when they sauntered down to the waterfront, and Judy nodded at the red beam of Pound O' Tea Light streaking across the silvered waters.

"I won't trade views for your gallows," she said.

31

"There are advantages to living here on the Foreside." She pointed to a big white house facing the harbor. "I'm staying at Captain Dunning's. He and his wife took me in because the captain's on the library board. Mrs. Matt even feeds me, except when I stay through like tonight."

"Don't gloat," Tim said sternly. "You'll be on a low-calorie diet next winter when I'm still a fine figger of a man. I know. I've sampled Mrs. Matt's cooking. She gave me a dish full of scalloped clams one night last week when Sandys Winter's car broke down and I drove him over here for supper." He cocked an eyebrow and studied Judy critically. "You know, if it's a view you want, I ought to drive you over to Gibbet Ridge now while you're still thin enough to fit into a Park Ford. Mr. Winter's the man who really has one."

"What's so different about his?" Judy asked, laughing.

"It's the combination he's got," Tim said. He waved his arm at the lobster boats and pleasure craft rocking at their moorings in the harbor. "The twentieth century on this side of him and the nineteenth on the other."

Judy looked bewildered. "Don't stop there," she ordered. "You've lost me. Where does the nineteenth century come in?"

"In a couple of schooners," Tim explained, "old fore-and-afters, the *Ellen B.* and the *Flying Nancy,* and a clipper called the *Golden Falcon.* Your Captain Matt's grandfather was master of the *Falcon,* and Captain Matt supervised the job of getting the three of them shipshape again for Mr. Winter. They just got towed in and anchored off Bold Dick Beach ten days ago." He squinted at his wristwatch in the moonlight. "It isn't ten yet. We still have time to row around them. How about it?"

But Judy stared over at the Park car suspiciously. Maybe he didn't wear snakes coiled around his waist but he'd already admitted he drove around with them. "It's the company you keep," she informed him. "And if you think I want to see *anything* enough to take a moonlight ride with Junior, the answer is a cinch: I don't!"

"Then what are we waiting for?" Tim demanded. "Sometime you'll catch on to how bright I am. I actually doped out your reaction to Junior yesterday. Besides, you hurt his feelings and he has to stay in bed."

## 4 · *The* Ellen B.

TIM jockeyed the car out of its parking slot and they headed back up Ship Street for Gallows Road.

"Even Miss Leonard's committee finally went home, I see," Judy said as they passed the dark buildings on the Mall, "but at the rate this town's concentrating on Bold Dick, he'll probably 'walk' before the summer's over! What do you do if you meet a ghost waving a cutlass? Use a silver bullet on him?"

"And get strung up on their gallows by the irate citizens?" Tim asked. "Any time I meet Bold Dick I say 'aye, aye, sir' and knuckle my forehead in a hurry."

"At least your uniform's green, not scarlet," Judy said with a comforting grin. "Maybe you'll survive—which is more than the citizens are likely to do before this celebration's over. Barry St. Leger is even putting on a musical version of *Rogue's Hour,* book and lyrics by Runner and Harne, no less. They're here already.

He had them with him in the library tonight, working like mad on costumes and scenery."

Tim whistled. "That's something we see," he announced with determination. "Don't make any other dates for Bold Dick Week till I find out what night I can get us tickets. Right?"

Judy nodded but she looked a bit skeptical. "*If* you can get us tickets, you mean," she amended. "This place is going to be snowed. Tourists will queue up outside that theater like the tail of a kite every time the box office is open."

"Then I'll wear my dirk in my teeth and elbow them aside," Tim assured her.

"Or you could take a few lessons in pocket picking," she suggested helpfully. "A dirk in your teeth must taste disgustingly metallic."

"Then I might as well save energy and just lean on the theater door," he said. "Unless its lock is different from all the others in this town, it'll swing open and I can help myself. What could be simpler?"

"I know," Judy agreed. "The lock on the library door would make a burglar laugh himself sick. I bet you could open it with a hairpin!"

"You probably could," Tim said placidly. "The trouble with you, Miss Carrington, is that you're a city slicker. Unless everything is nailed down, you expect the worst."

"Maybe," she said. "Just the same, that library owns the longhand draft of *Rogue's Hour* and goodness knows how many other valuable manuscripts, Tim. I found eight of them tonight when I was straightening up. Stuck casually in file drawers! There weren't any locks on them either, and the names on those manuscripts sounded like a course in American lit. You can argue all you want, but I still think it would make more sense if Mr. Winter had built in a few burglarproof cabinets instead of some of those office-workshops he put in that wing for Sinnett Harbor's literary lights!"

"It would make sense to me, too," Tim admitted. "I'm another city slicker. It wouldn't hurt my feelings if he put a few good locks on his own place either. Every time he goes away I wonder why he expects to find anything when he comes back."

"And in his New York apartment he probably has one of those safety steel bars that run from a slot in the floor up against the door," Judy exclaimed.

"Sure, he does," Tim said, "but around here a locked door only means the family's gone calling or the shop's closed for the night. It isn't supposed to keep out burglars. Sinnet Harbor's never had any, so Mr. Winter doesn't bother to worry. It's the Ranger Station that gets the jitters. We haven't seen anything yet in his house, except the kitchen sink, that couldn't be peddled at a fancy price to some museum."

"You mean you're supposed to keep an eye on his place, too?" Judy asked in surprise. "I should think you'd have all you could handle with those cabins."

"You wouldn't get far selling that idea to the Chief Ranger," Tim said drily. "When a man gives the land for a national park and then makes a will adding his house and its contents for a maritime museum, the Chief figures the whole works is our responsibility. You can't hate him for that either. The three ships are our newest babies. They're part of the museum project."

"No wonder there's a Winter-ish aura over Sinnett Harbor," Judy said thoughtfully. "A park, a museum, and a library wing! He doesn't exactly hand out peanuts, does he? What's he really like, Tim? I've seen his picture often enough, but I've been wondering ever since I hit this place."

"Maine Yankee covers it," Tim said. "Salty and independent, though I guess he isn't too rugged any more. He's seventy-eight, and the Chief says he had some kind of heart attack in November. You'd never know it from him, though. He hates having people fuss over him. Not that that gets him anywhere with his housekeeper, Elvira Snow." Tim's grin grew wide. "Elvira inherited Mr. Winter. She was his mother's last 'hired girl' and she says she aims to keep him and the house in the same shape his mother left them."

He turned the Ford in between the Park gateposts and flapped his hand at the Ranger Station. "Mr. Winter's house was still there where our quarters are when his mother died, and according to one of Captain Matt's yarns, Elvira Snow sat tight in her rocking chair in the kitchen the whole time it took to move it down to the Ridge. That's the house, Judy, just ahead of us where the road stops. Bold Dick's Anchorage is off to the left."

He parked by a clump of bayberry and gave her a

hand out. "Good night! I didn't even warn you about heels. Can you make it? From here on in, there's only a path."

Judy held a slender foot out in the moonlight. "Shells," she said, nonchalantly. "Lead on, Ranger. I'm the Tall Gal type."

But when the path sloped down to the beach, her feet shot out from under her, and she landed ignominiously in Tim's arms.

"Just about the right height, at that," he remarked, smiling at her. "Almost to the top of my nose."

"Then I'll remember not to eat the wrong side of the mushroom like Alice in Wonderland," Judy promised demurely, but she pushed herself back on her own feet in a hurry and got busy helping launch the skiff.

"We're heading for the *Ellen B.*," Tim told her as they rowed across the path of the moon. "She's not as beautiful as the *Golden Falcon*—the raking spars of that clipper would be hard to beat—but she's an interesting old gal. She's practically a twin of Bold Dick's *Sea Hawk*."

Shipping his oars, he let the skiff drift in toward the sturdy hull of the old schooner, and Judy studied it curiously.

"I wonder how anyone knows," she speculated. "Would it be from the design, Tim?"

"That would tell an expert like Captain Matt," he said, nodding, "but the captain didn't have to do any brooding over this one. His ancestors built both ships, and he has their specifications in the old shipyard records. Besides, Mr. Winter has an oil painting of the *Sea Hawk,* done the year she finally went down off the Grand Banks, and the *Ellen*'s a dead ringer for her. There were only five years between the end of the *Sea Hawk* and the launching of the *Ellen.* This tough old lady dates back to 1830."

Judy caught her breath. "A hundred and twenty-five years and still afloat!" she said, awed.

"Well, the *Constitution* and the *Charles Morgan* are still afloat, too," Tim reminded her. "The *Morgan* had been chasing whales for eighty years when she retired in 1921, and *Old Ironsides* fought in the War of 1812. If a Yankee built a ship, he put backbone in her."

"You can say *that* again," Judy conceded, but she raised a quizzical eyebrow as she looked from the old schooner back to Tim. "I'm drinking all this in avidly," she assured him. "Only curiosity is killing me. I thought you were a snake man! How come the seagoing lore?"

"Captain Matt," Tim admitted, grinning. "The Chief got him to come over here and lecture to us so we wouldn't sound like morons about 'iron men and wooden ships.' We took notes, no less. Just scratch me anywhere and I'll exude information!" They were rowing past the *Golden Falcon*'s figurehead on their way back to the beach, and he nodded up at her lofty spars. "Get your landlord to show you the scale model of this clipper he's building for Mr. Winter, Judy. He brought it over here to use for demonstration, and its rigging drove us all plain nuts."

"So that's what Miss Leonard meant when she said Captain Matt's hobby was ship models," Judy exclaimed. "I thought she meant he just collected them."

"It's the other way around," Tim assured her. "People collect his—and how! When you get aboard the *Ellen* sometime, take a look at a little model of a fishing schooner with a nest of dories on her deck. It's one of his, and a yachtsman over in the Harbor offered eight hundred dollars for it last week. All I hope is that some light-fingered tourist doesn't get a notion that it'd make a swell souvenir."

## 5 · The Shadow at the Window

TIM gave the oars a last vigorous dip that sent the skiff grating onto the beach, and they clambered over the bow to haul it up above high-water mark before they tramped back across the sand. This time Judy made it safely along the slope to the path on the Ridge, but she lingered a minute for a last look at the wooden ships in the old pirate anchorage.

"The shadow of the past is long in Sinnett Harbor," she said dreamily. "Thanks for bringing me over, Tim. In this moonlight I can almost see Bold Dick's buccaneers swarming up the rigging to put to sea again. Maybe we should have hoisted the Jolly Roger on the *Ellen* when we were out there. I never will forgive Charity Royalle for turning her pirate into the owner of a fleet of fishing schooners and making him die respectably in bed. I shall go and make a face at her headstone behind the Parish Church first thing tomorrow."

41

"A fine upstanding citizen you turned out to be," Tim said severely. "I'm glad I didn't take you aboard the *Ellen*. Next thing I'd have been walking the plank, and your 'shadow of the past' is long enough around here now to suit me. Last night some joker fastened a dummy on that dratted gallows at the crossroads, and I nearly passed out."

"I would have," Judy told him promptly. "I like my pirates live and kicking with brass rings in their ears, not 'sun-dried' on a gibbet. Maybe that thing's picturesque, but it gave me melancholia in broad daylight."

"Well, it didn't faze Elvira Snow any," Tim said chuckling. "She came up to the mailbox and stopped to watch me cut the dummy down. Apparently boys pull that stunt so often that she takes it in her stride— though she did allow that this one almost gave her 'a turn.' She said she thought it was Peleg Gillen who keeps the lobster pound over at the wharf, until she remembered his wife wouldn't let him make off with that much new rope just to hang himself! According to Elvira, Captain Peleg's mighty nigh, but his wife is nigher."

"Oh dear, I hope the library's on Elvira Snow's visiting list," Judy said. "She sounds as if she'd brighten our days."

"Don't worry; you'll meet her," Tim told her. "She stops by every now and then when she drives over to the village to market. Ever since Mr. Winter won the Pulitzer Prize she keeps a sharp eye on modern fiction.

She wants to know whether the new choices measure up. Elvira is not one to lower her sights."

"But what does she do when Mr. Winter's away?" Judy asked. "She certainly can't stay here alone."

"She certainly can," Tim insisted. "I guess she has one of her cronies stay for a while when he goes to Hollywood or New York for a couple of months. Otherwise she holds the fort herself. Elvira's ten or a dozen years younger than Mr. Winter. Not that that makes her any spring chicken," he added candidly, "but she's spry enough to make most people pant."

Judy shook her head as she swung around to look along the path at the big white house beyond the pines. "Not for me," she told him. "I'd have goose-bumps. It's too lonesome and shadowy even in moonlight. Imagine what it's like when the fog rolls in!"

"It's lonesome," Tim agreed. "The Ranger Station's out of sight up by the gate and the nearest cabins are over a mile in the other direction. But you can't blame Mr. Winter for not wanting them any closer. Some of the barbershop quartets around campfires in this Park at night would make a coyote envious. At least his Ridge stays quiet and peaceful."

From force of habit Tim's glance roamed over the shrubbery around the big house near the water, and suddenly Judy felt him stiffen. "Or does it?" he muttered in an odd voice.

Turning in surprise, she watched him squeeze his eyes tight as if to clear them and then stare fixedly at the house again.

43

"Take a look, too, will you, Judy?" he asked. "I thought I spotted a queer shadow under that first window—the one at this end on the first floor."

Following his pointing finger, Judy looked blank. "I don't see a thing," she began. Then she stopped in dismay. "Yes I do! Only—your shadow's not under the window now, Tim. It's twisted right across the pane!"

"I see it," Tim said quietly. "I'll be back as soon as I can, Judy. I've got to get over there."

He gave her a fleeting smile as he started to run, but Judy had no intention of being abandoned. "I'm not as useless as I look," she panted indignantly at his heels. "If I had to throw a book at a rattlesnake yesterday, I might as well throw something at a mere man!"

"A *pine* snake," Tim said automatically, and Judy grinned between gasps. What a guy. If he were going down for the third time, he'd manage a last word to straighten you out on sea serpents!

They were clear of the last pines now, and he pulled her up for a quick survey. Ahead of them loomed the field-stone wall that separated Gibbet Ridge from the rest of Gun Point, but over it they could still see a dark shadow against the window.

"What's he trying to do?" Judy demanded in a puzzled whisper. "At least, I suppose that thing's a man. Right now it looks more like a humpbacked spider!" There was such obvious distaste in her voice that Tim gave her hand a reassuring pressure.

"It's a man all right," he said quietly, "a man with a knife in his hand. See the moonlight glint on the

44

blade? He's trying to slip it in to turn the latch, but he can keep at that till kingdom come without getting anywhere. Mr. Winter's windows are so old they don't even have latches. The upper sashes are fixed and the lower ones have metal catches built in the frame. They can't be budged from the outside."

"Then maybe if he's that frustrated we can sneak up on him before he knows it," Judy suggested, but Tim shook his head.

"Not in this moonlight. He's bound to look around once in a while. And if it comes to playing hide and seek with a guy with a knife, you stay back against the wall away from the shrubbery. That's an order, Judy."

"I'll stay put," she promised. "It certainly won't help any if you start stewing about me, too."

Relieved, he gave her fingers another quick pressure, and they started on, more cautiously this time, and slipped through a narrow gate flanked by lilacs and along the inner side of the wall.

To Judy, even the slight crunch of a twig under her feet seemed thunderous, but the twisted shadow at the window seemed utterly unconcerned. Nobody could be stupid enough not to keep his ears open, she thought incredulously. He must be stone deaf! Then Tim's fingers touched hers again, warning her to a standstill, and she was straining to catch his words.

"I'm off," he whispered. "Keep your eyes on him, Judy, and whistle when he bolts."

Nodding, she shrank back against the wall, and braced herself to watch and wait. Something had to happen soon. Caution tossed overboard, Tim was pounding across the grass, making for the bushes under that end window. Not even a deaf man could miss the noise much longer. And their shadow was not missing it! Like the shifting pieces in a kaleidoscope, the picture dissolved before her eyes, and her whistle rang shrill over Gibbet Ridge. With a last grotesque twist, the shadow had vanished.

Her eyes fixed on Tim plunging into the barricade of shrubbery around the house, Judy yanked ruthlessly at one of the wooden poles staking hollyhocks along the wall. She had no idea which way that shadow was heading. She only wanted something good and long and hard in her hand. Eyes and ears alert, she edged closer to the gateway. At least, if he made a break for that, she could stick out her pole to trip him and yell for Tim.

She shivered, though, as she listened to the sounds from the shrubbery, following Tim's route by the wild motion of the branches. Chasing someone you could see was not so bad, but struggling through bushes after a hidden man with a knife was horrible. If only the prowler would decide to make a run for it. Then suddenly tense, she faded closer to the wall, her heart thudding. Something seemed to be moving at the corner of the house, and it wasn't Tim! She could still see branches threshing down the side of the house. Straining her eyes, she waited, motionless. She must be absolutely sure before she called. Tim needed all his

46

wits about him beating through those bushes. She dare not risk dividing his attention.

But she was sure now. A dark shape was creeping out of the bamboos close to the pillars of the porch, and her voice rose urgently. "Tim! Tim! Around front, quick."

For a split second the figure wavered, its head darting over its shoulder, and Judy's voice rose again in an involuntary cry of horror. That twisted, crouching thing scuttling out of the moonlight had no face!

"Judy! Are you all right? Judy!" Tim tore back up the garden, and she flung herself at him headlong.

"I'm all right; just keep on going," she begged. "He's cut across to the other side of the house."

Sensibly, Tim did not stop to ask questions. He started off again on the double, but he seized Judy's hand and pulled her after him.

"This time I want you where I can see you," he said grimly. "For a guy who asked a girl for a moonlight row, I'm sure doing fine!"

## 6 · The Man from Gibbet Ridge

JUDY did not delay action by arguing. She was more than willing to be under Tim's eye. Besides, she had already learned that keeping up with a ranger in a hurry took all her wind. She could tell her story later. Right now she had to concentrate on running, and save her breath. But from the tail of her eye as they pelted past the house, she thought she saw a light flash on downstairs, and she almost cried out. They had been making enough racket in the last ten minutes to wake Rip Van Winkle, and Mr. Winter had a bad heart! Worried, she tried to turn her head for a second look, and promptly crashed into Tim skidding to an unexpected stop.

"How dumb can I get?" he panted. "The Bay, Judy! I never even think of it, and he makes off in a boat. Listen! You can hear his oars."

Judy, however, was shaking his arm frantically. As long as that faceless thing was gone, she didn't care whether it used a boat or a helicopter.

"The house," she wheezed. "Lights. We've waked Mr. Winter."

But she had barely struggled the words out before a window banged up, and a disturbed voice hailed them.

"What's going on around here?" it demanded. "Who's out there?"

"It's Tim Wade, Mr. Winter," Tim answered quickly. "I'll be right over to report."

"Oh, it's you, is it, Ranger?" The voice sounded re-assured. "Come around to the front door, then, and I'll let you in."

The window slammed down again, and they plodded toward the house.

"You must be bushed, Judy," Tim said contritely. "I certainly dragged you into something. Next time I'll case the whole Park before I bring you over."

He sounded so tired and disgusted that Judy managed to conjure up a feeble grin. "At least, I've never been less bored on a date in my life," she pointed out, and he smiled back at her with frank admiration.

"Just remind me and I'll stage a holdup for you on my next night off," he promised. "All you have to do is save Friday. Will you, Judy?"

"I can hardly wait," she informed him. "After to-night and yesterday, it'd be awful to have this Park go dull on me!"

But even at midnight Gun Point was not quite through surprising her, and she blinked in confused astonishment as Tim presented her to the man waiting for them in the doorway of the rambling white house.

He might be wearing a tailor-made robe now, but the last time she saw him he was dressed in fishy dungarees and hip rubber boots. Her lobsterman of the stalled Model A was Sandys Winter. And if he really was a stuffed shirt underneath, in spite of what Tim had said, he'd never forgive her for not recognizing him even in disguise!

Judy need not have bothered to worry, however. Mr. Winter was already greeting her with cordial friendliness, his eyes twinkling slightly at her startled expression.

"Miss Carrington and I have met after a fashion," he told Tim. "She was kind enough to give my Ford a push on Gallows Road yesterday. But, of course, then I had the advantage of her," he added with a tactful courtesy that won Judy completely. "The bookmobile told me she must be our new library assistant, and my stalled car didn't help her a bit."

Leading the way into a comfortable living room, he pulled forward a pair of chairs and they sank down gratefully.

"Now tell me what happened, Ranger. Something that sounded like a shout suddenly roused me, and I find you dragging our newest staff member after you like a Neanderthal man. Should I be registering a protest?"

"We were chasing after somebody trying to get in one of your windows, Mr. Winter," Tim explained, "and I was idiot enough to leave Judy alone by the stone wall while I beat the bushes." His jaw tightened. "She hasn't had time to tell me what happened yet but something scared her. That's why I dragged her with me the rest of the time. The man gave us the slip anyway. He had a skiff on your shore."

Sandys Winter stared at Tim in consternation. "Did you have to leave Miss Carrington with a prowler loose on the Ridge?" he asked in horrified disapproval.

"But I had to stay alone somewhere, Mr. Winter," Judy said. "Tim was chasing through the shrubbery after a man with a knife. He just thought I'd be safer by the stone wall; we both did."

Mr. Winter looked considerably startled. "I guess you were at that," he admitted, but his blue eyes studied Judy shrewdly. "I don't think you scare very easily, Miss Carrington. What happened to make you yell like that? By now I'm prepared for anything."

"So am I," Tim said promptly. "I saw Judy tackle what she thought was a rattlesnake yesterday, and there's nothing wrong with her nerve. If she yelled, she had a reason for it."

"I was scared half out of my wits," Judy confessed frankly. "That man came creeping out of the bushes all twisted up like his own shadow. And he didn't have any face! You were halfway to the wall, Tim, before I even had sense enough to realize he had a mask on."

Both men were listening, as taken aback as Judy had been. "A black handkerchief over his face maybe," Tim muttered in bewilderment, and Mr. Winter nodded.

"That puts a different light on the performance," he

said thoughtfully. "Are you sure about that mask, Miss Carrington?"

"I'm afraid I am," Judy said reluctantly. "He wasn't more than twelve feet beyond me, and the moonlight was on him. The mask means he was somebody who thought he'd be recognized, doesn't it? Somebody local?"

"I guess it does," Sandys Winter said, sighing. "Change is inevitable, I suppose, but Sinnett Harbor has retained its hard Yankee core of integrity a long time."

"There's something wrong with the whole picture, though," Tim protested. "This man thought your house was empty. That's for sure. He was taking his own sweet time and he didn't expect to be interrupted. But I'd be willing to bet that even Judy knew you got home on the 6:30 A.M. train from New York yesterday, and she's been in Sinnett Harbor exactly three days!"

"You'd collect," Judy assured him promptly. "Before we've finished breakfast, the postman has already told Mrs. Matt who's left and who's arrived on the first two trains, and the expressman and the parcel-postman between them carry the library staff clear through the 4:10. I heard about Mr. Winter's being home every hour on the hour yesterday. My goodness, even the telephone operators tell you who's in and who's out and where they've gone. I tried to call Captain Matt for Miss Leonard after lunch today, and the operator said there wasn't any use ringing because the Dunnings had just driven off down the Dyer's Cove Road! I guess if that man's local, we can start looking for somebody deaf, dumb, and blind."

The novelist chuckled at her vivid sketch of his home town's grapevine. "You've got something there," he said more cheerfully. "I feel better already. Even out here on the Ridge we keep pretty well up to date. Perhaps a mask is this particular burglar's trademark. Anyway, whoever the man was, I'm grateful to you both for coming to the rescue of my property." His eyes began to twinkle again as he walked to the door with them. "Maybe you'd better come back and rescue *me* tomorrow. I just this minute remembered Elvira Snow! She's grown a bit hard of hearing, and I've let her sleep through the only excitement Gibbet Ridge has had since the 'Hue and Cry' boys caught a horse thief a hundred years ago."

## 7 · The Day After the Night Before

JUDY opened one eye and glared balefully at the alarm clock when it went off next morning. She had finally crawled into bed at two in the morning, and the thought of radiating intelligence at a reference desk all day made her moan. "What that library should have hired was a cross between Little Annie Oakley and a lady snake charmer," she grumbled. Considering everything, she was sure it was nothing less than a miracle that she could even fumble into her bathrobe and stagger down the hall to the shower.

She revived sufficiently over doughnuts and clam-cakes and coffee, however, to give Captain and Mrs. Matt a spirited account of the events on Gibbet Ridge.

"Tim Wade's still growling over not collaring whoever it was," she finished, "but it certainly wasn't his fault he didn't. He plowed through every bush around the place. Even I turned myself into a roadblock, and all the time that man had come by water!"

Captain Matt's jaw dropped. "Heave to there a minute, Judy," he ordered. "What kind of a boat?"

"Just a rowboat," she said.

"And you couldn't identify the cut of his jib again, you say?" he persisted.

Judy shook her head. "Not a chance," she told him. "He had that handkerchief over his face, and he skittered along all scrunched up like a gigantic insect. I don't even know whether he was tall or short. He might actually be deformed for all I could tell, though somehow I don't think so. I haven't any logical reason for it. I just have a feeling he was scooting along crouched and twisted that way for his own purposes. Why, Captain Matt? You don't think he's going to hang around, do you? I still don't believe he belongs in Sinnett Harbor."

The captain looked regretful. "It doesn't seem likely," he admitted. "Only my skiff's turned up missing this morning. I'd like to lay my hands on him; that's all."

Judy gulped. "And book reviewers have the nerve to fuss about coincidence," she exclaimed. "After this, I'll believe anything."

"More convenience than coincidence," Captain Matt answered. "That skiff was just handy like a sitting duck. There's a mess of them over at the yacht club, but you have to have a key to get through the door to the club wharf, and Peleg Gillen, being Peleg, keeps his chained to his lobster car."

"Now, Matt, he's treasurer of the library board," his wife said mildly. "You'll give Judy a fine impression." But there were laughter crinkles around her eyes in spite of her good intentions, and her irrepressible husband smiled broadly.

"Better eat another one of those clamcakes to bolster your strength, Jen," he advised her. "Until that skiff turns up somewhere, Peleg and Maybelle Gillen are going to jaw your ear off for not keeping me closer hauled."

"I've already heard about the Gillens," Judy reassured Mrs. Dunning, laughing. "I didn't know Captain Peleg was on the library board, but otherwise Captain Matt didn't give a thing away. Was he really a captain, too, or is that just a courtesy title?"

"Freighter captain," her landlord said promptly. "We were in the same class at the Maritime Academy down to Castine. Peleg was a comforting man on a bridge in bad weather, but his crew seemed a mite on the lean side." He cocked his head and considered his classmate again. "Old Doc Holliday swears Peleg was born pinching a couple of pennies till they squawked," he said thoughtfully, "and the Doc was there. He ought to know. But I still figure Peleg might have studied to be pretty near human if Maybelle had never learned to cipher."

Judy thought of the contrast between the two captains when she passed the Gillen lobster pound a few minutes later on her way to work. She enjoyed listening to the yarns about Captain Peleg, though she was beginning to wonder how Miss Leonard managed to buy books with such a lavish hand. But she thanked her lucky stars that her room was at Captain Matt's. So far, having breakfast with the Dunnings seemed likely to give any day a lift. Now all she needed to top the morning off was a quiet, orderly routine at the library for a change.

She had no more than reached the building, however, before she realized she was not destined to get it. Two vans from Portland were backed up outside, disgorging furniture for the new wing, and the place was in a state of upheaval. Besides, it did not take five minutes to discover that Bold Dick fever was still raging in epidemic proportions. Barry St. Leger and his stage designer arrived and went into a huddle, surrounded by books on period furniture. Reporters from the *Harbor Breeze* kept wanting to know where to find town histories and files of earlier newspapers. Four determined magazine writers each demanded the library's only remaining volume on Maine folkways, and tourists, already swarming like locusts for the coming celebration, popped in and out asking for *Rogue's Hour*. By two o'clock there was not a single copy of the book on the shelves and by three-thirty there was no other Sandys Winter title either.

"Maybe we could cancel the children's story period Saturday and tell *Rogue's Hour*," Judy said hopefully when she located Miss Leonard on a ladder in the new browsing room. "Think of the work it would save. About now all I could dream up was to send people over to Gun Point Park for a look at the *Ellen B*. The rangers are going to adore me!"

"You'd better run over to the Sea Serpent and see if

our new copies have arrived yet," Miss Leonard decided. "They're supposed to be charged to the library, Judy, and if they aren't in, you tell Nate Josselyn for me that I expect a dozen copies from his stock. He ordered them practically by the carload. It won't hurt him to part with a few."

Judy nodded. "Can do," she said with alacrity, and vanished in the direction of the staff room and her lipstick before anything happened to make Miss Leonard change her mind.

Ship Street wore a leisurely midafternoon air when she turned out of the Mall ten minutes later, and she rambled along in a mood to match it. After being inside all day, she would have been quite willing to learn that Nate Josselyn had suddenly moved his bookshop, lock, stock, and barrel, a couple of blocks farther from the library. She could already see the salty sea serpent ahump on its swinging wooden sign, however, and she crossed the street dutifully. This was her first chance to get inside the Sea Serpent, and she was curious about the place. According to the stories at the library, Josselyn's served as a sort of club for the writers in Sinnett Harbor's summer colony. Apparently the semicircle of chairs in front of its fireplace was occupied most of the time, and the room was blue with pipe smoke.

Judy smiled to herself as she headed for the door. The pungent fragrance of tobacco was drifting out to meet her. Those chairs must be full. If she hadn't already made a fine botch of recognizing Sandys Winter, whose picture had been staring at her from book jackets all her life, she could play "Authors" to amuse herself while she waited for her books. It's a good thing I'm not going in for bank telling, she thought wryly. If a bandit just changed his haircut, I'd think he was a new customer and let him rob me all over again! Obviously there wasn't any use in spraining her brain. Authors dressed for dust-jacket photographs were a different breed of cats from authors in fishing clothes.

Once inside, however, Judy promptly got involved in mental gymnastics. A man who stopped beside her a minute on his way out looked so irritatingly half-familiar that she forgot even to glance toward the fireplace until the clerk suddenly reappeared with her package. Then she came to in a hurry, thoroughly disgusted with herself, and found Mr. Winter leaning against the counter, laughing at her.

"It's lucky we're going your way," he said with amusement. "You'd never make it across Ship Street alone. Sam Runner's been waving his pipe at you for the last five minutes!"

"I was spraining my brain again," Judy said sadly. "Not that it did me much good, though. The more I tried to remember, the better I forgot. Maybe I need one of those concentration courses. You know: 'Why, it's Mr. Addison Sims from Seattle.' "

"Who wants to remember Mr. Sims anyway?" Sandys Winter asked cheerfully. He waved at the two men bearing down on them, and Judy's eyes sparkled with triumph.

"Don't tell me! This time I know," she said. "The

man with Mr. Runner is Glen Teed, isn't he, Mr. Winter? The woman in the other half of my seat on the train last Sunday was reading him, and I looked at his picture practically all the way from New York to Sinnett Harbor!"

"You should be flattered, Glen," Mr. Winter remarked as the playwright introduced his companion to Judy and the four of them strolled out the door together. "Miss Carrington knew you on sight."

"Who says crime doesn't pay?" Sam Runner demanded. "We want to enlist your services anyway, Miss Carrington. This man arrived last night, a week early for the wing-dings, and he hasn't a thing to do except get in our hair. You can feed him clues. What's the use of a mystery writer if he can't catch Sand Winter's burglar for him?"

"Maybe he could begin by finding Captain Matt's skiff," Judy suggested, smiling. Stopping in front of the library to retrieve her package from Mr. Teed's arm, she smiled up at him gratefully. She thought she was fairly tall herself, but she felt small beside the mystery writer's six feet three. "Mr. Winter's prowler borrowed it last night, and it hasn't come home to roost. You never can tell. There might be incriminating fingerprints all over the oar handles."

## 8 · *The Altruistic Mr. Teed*

ACTUALLY, before forty-eight hours had passed, Captain Matt had found his skiff for himself. It had been abandoned three miles down shore.

"You tell your young ranger he must have dampened that sculpin's spirits considerable," the captain told Judy at supper Thursday night. "He rowed clear to the town limits before he took to his heels. It looks as if he figured they'd appreciate his talents better down at Dyer's Cove."

"That news certainly won't hurt Tim's feelings," Judy said. "When he called up yesterday, he said he was stuck with night guard duty on Gibbet Ridge for the rest of the week! The Chief Ranger must have been in a tizzy, because with only four rangers, they've never tried to cover the place like that before. Anyway, Mr. Winter will be happy. His house being nearly robbed didn't bother him half as much as the chance that man came from Sinnett Harbor."

61

She set her coffee cup down and looked at the Dunnings thoughtfully. "I'm already changing my mind about my mother's not recognizing the Harbor anymore. That 'hard Yankee core of integrity' she and Mr. Winter talk about is still pretty healthy, and that's what gives the place its character. As far as I can see, the changes on Ship Street don't really mean a thing. They're only on the surface."

"Just face lifting," Mrs. Matt agreed, smiling at her. "For three or four months the tempo's livelier; that's about all. Then we settle down again with our livers nicely stirred up." Her chuckle grew reminiscent. "Of course, some folks complain that summer people are full of crotchets, but personally I prefer my liver stirred up by them than by my grandmother's doses of sulphur and molasses! I shouldn't wonder any either, Judy, if your mother would, too. Your grandmother Mariner used to drench every youngster in the family with catnip tea and pennyroyal."

But whatever new-fangled contours its face lifting had given Sinnett Harbor, its grapevine announced the return of Captain Matt's skiff with such old-fashioned efficacy that word had spread to Gun Point by noon. On a flying trip to town during Judy's lunch hour, Tim tore into the library long enough to report that night patrol was off and their date on again.

"Only we postpone that holdup I promised you till next time," he told her. "Tonight we just celebrate, and we celebrate on Ship Street, where lights are bright and burglars don't burgle. Don't forget to tell Mrs.

62

Matt you won't be in for supper. We're starting at the Whistling Clam."

And when Tim said celebrate, he meant it, Judy discovered. The shore dinner at the Clam was only the beginning. They took in the first show at the movies, skidded up the gangplank of the *Harbor Viking* just in time for a moonlight cruise of Pentecost Bay, and only landed on the Dunning doorstep at 1 A.M. because Clem Doughty's bowling alleys inconsiderately closed at 12:45. For a while Judy even thought they were going to get through a whole evening without a single reference to snakes, but that was before the short at the Bayview turned out to be a wildlife picture of the Everglades. After that, assorted reptiles crawled in and out of the conversation for the duration of their date.

Over the weekend, though, with Tim on duty, Judy did not have to concentrate on anything that crawled except the lobsters at the library board's clambake for the staff, and concentrating on lobsters was no trouble at all. In fact, she did not give snakes another thought until Tim's book on Brazilian antivenoms arrived in Monday's parcel post. Then she hastily catalogued it herself, and plopped it beside her on the front seat of the bookmobile when she started on her Park rounds after lunch. Encountering Elvira Snow in the stacks that morning and clam-baking with Captain Peleg the day before had put her in a fine gossipy mood, and she hoped she would find Tim perched on the porch railing when she stopped at the Ranger Station with his book.

However, nobody even answered her energetic honks,

63

and she drove on past, intent on finishing her route in record time and saying good-bye to her favorite tow-headed cub. This first contingent of boys would be gone when she made her next trip and she was going to miss young Jimmy Merrill's happy grin. But at the cub camp site she learned she would not have long to miss him.

"I'm sorry he's out, Miss Carrington," the cubmaster said. "He's shadowing Ranger Wade as usual. I'll give him your messages, but you haven't seen the last of him, you know. His parents have rented a cabin for the rest of the summer, and he'll be back in a week or so. The kid had a bout with polio late last fall, luckily a mild one, and his dad thinks this outdoor life is putting the finishing touches on his cure. Jimmy's father is a well-known orthopedic surgeon, by the way."

"That's a relief," Judy said with a smile. "Judging from his son's tastes, I'd have guessed Dr. Merrill was curator of reptiles for some zoo. Now I won't have to dodge pet specimens around their doorstep!"

"That's what you think," the cubmaster retorted cheerily. "See those four cages over there? They house three different kinds of snakes and a two-toed salamander. Ranger Wade is enlisted to take charge till Jimmy comes back. After that, you start dodging." He chuckled at her wry expression. "The ranger and Jimmy are sure two of a kind," he remarked. "Have you seen that baby dragon Wade calls a pet?"

"Seen him!" Judy exclaimed. "I practically stepped on him the first day I hit this Park, and I nearly headed back for the New York Public Library. I haven't got

64

out of the bookmobile at the Ranger Station since."

Just the same, when it came to leaving the book about Brazilian antivenoms at the Station on her way off Gun Point, Judy reluctantly decided to take one more chance. The building seemed to be deserted again. At least, no one paid any attention to the prolonged blast of her horn, and she finally climbed out of the bookmobile, feeling like an early Christian martyr about to be thrown to the lions. From somewhere around the rear of the log cabin, she thought she heard a few faint sounds, but she had already had her fill of the entrance in the back ell. If she had to approach the place at all, she was sticking to the front path where there were no bushes to harbor Junior. She was willing to give him credit for being nonpoisonous, but that credit did not cover his slithering in her direction.

Judy's progress toward the steps, moreover, was distinctly hesitant until she sighted the pine snake's screened box on the porch, with the whittled stick properly fitted through the hasp on its lid. Then she stepped out almost nonchalantly. She even peered into the box as she banged the knocker. Caged up that way, Junior was not so appalling. Besides, she had suddenly thought of a perfect use for him: with all those black patches on his white skin, he'd make an absolutely stunning shoulder bag! Chuckling at the idea of Tim's face if she came up with that suggestion, she banged the knocker once more before she gave up. Anyway, this time she had the ideal place to leave a book on antivenoms for snake bites.

Junior hissed indignantly when she leaned over his

cage, but she refused to let that stop her. "From me to you with malice," she said gleefully, and parked the book on top of his box just as the door opened beside her.

"Now why are you throwing books at him?" Tim's voice demanded, and Judy managed to look pained.

"All I was doing was taking hissing lessons," she announced. "I don't know which side of your family Junior takes after, Tim Wade, but he certainly has a nasty temper!"

"On the touchy side," Tim agreed judicially. "He was born with a neurosis. His mother was frightened by a brown-eyed blonde, too."

"Stop trying to confuse the issue," Judy ordered with a grin. "We were talking about hostile personalities in the Wade family. After all, *you* frightened our prowling pal clear out of town." She smiled at him happily. "And speaking of him, I met Elvira Snow in the library this morning and she's tops. No wonder Mr. Winter's characters are full of flavor. All he has to do is listen to Elvira."

"The admiration is mutual," Tim assured her. "Jimmy Merrill and I split some kindling on the Ridge this afternoon, and Elvira informed us you were not the usual modern flibbertigibbet. I was practically bowled over. Coming from Elvira Snow, lady, that is *praise*."

"My ego will be inflated for days," Judy admitted, looking pleased. But her feeling of satisfaction was promptly diluted by the pine snake. He was hissing again as he uncoiled a yard of length. "I just wish Elvira would point out my sterling character to Junior," she exclaimed. "He still doesn't appreciate me."

"No use," Tim told her. "He hasn't any ears. Still I could wangle a couple of hours off tonight and come get you," he added hopefully. "Then he could smell out your virtues for himself."

"Bold Dick Week coming up and rangers talk about time off, no less," Judy groaned. "What's the matter with *your* boss? The state mine's in, all three of us *and* the page will start sleeping in the library tomorrow!"

"Well, it was a good idea," Tim said sadly, "but I might have known I'd end up putting books away at a library."

"And that would be the pay-off," Judy retorted with fine ingratitude. "If that's your idea of helping, Ranger Wade, you can stay right here and baby-sit with Junior. Absolutely all we need about now is *Tom Sawyer* stuck in with the snake books."

But by Friday night when she found him leaning placidly against the reference desk a few minutes before closing time, she had another tune ready.

"You're practically the answer to prayer," she said joyfully. "And you needn't look so suspicious either! I was never so glad to see anyone with some sense before."

"Don't tell me; just let me guess," Tim said with resignation. "It couldn't be, could it, that I am about to *work?*"

"You mean you will?" Judy demanded. "Then for goodness' sake, come on." She dashed to put the lock on the door and began to steer him toward the new wing. "Frankly, if I have to cope with Glen Teed much longer, I'll go scatty."

"Isn't that the *Midnight Means Murder* guy?" Tim inquired. "He just moved into a Park cabin. Mr. Winter says he has a new book coming out that's going to wow 'em. Sold to the movies already. Who put him to work?"

"Nobody," Judy said succinctly. "He's altruistic." Then she looked conscience-stricken. "I really am an unappreciative heel," she said. "The poor man came over to do research on a new book and he hasn't accomplished a thing. Right in the middle of setting up exhibits for the open house after the dedication next Monday, Miss Addison fell off a ladder and he and Miss Leonard took her to the doctor. Then he came back to help *me!*"

Tim's eyebrows shot up. "By putting *Tom Sawyer* in with the snake books?" he asked, and Judy grinned.

"Okay, you win," she said, "but if I'd known what I know now, I'd have suggested it! The first thing he did was to drop a manuscript package from Mr. Winter's literary agents hard enough to burst it wide open and scatter pages all over the floor. I still don't see how he managed it. Honestly, Tim, the man's all thumbs. Right now I've got him setting up a bookmaking exhibit. I couldn't see what harm he'd do if he dropped a few galley sheets or some unbound pages, but he wants to help put Captain Matt's ship models on shelves in the browsing room! Do you wonder I'm glad to see you?

They're only lent to us for Bold Dick Week and they're worth a small fortune!"

"All right," Tim said. "You keep him talking, and I'll manage the models."

"I can try," Judy said dubiously. "Just the same, I almost wish you'd brought Junior. If he rattled his tail once, we wouldn't have any problem."

At the moment, however, they did not have a problem anyway. The book exhibit was neatly set up in the browsing room, but Mr. Teed had disappeared.

"Now where the dickens has he got to?" Judy exclaimed. "He hasn't gone home. That's his jacket on the back of the chair over there." For a moment she looked worried. Then she shrugged. "Oh, well, let's count our blessings. Those empty shelves are for the models, Tim. Let's hurry."

"Can't," Tim said laconically. He was counting the ships. "There are fifty of them, Judy, and we've got to figure out some arrangement. It's lucky they're labeled and dated or I wouldn't know the *Santa Maria* from a whaler."

"I wouldn't either," she admitted. "Why don't you put modern boats top and bottom and old ones in between? Bold Dick Week's supposed to celebrate the past, and people can see sailboats and cruisers around here every day. Of course, that three-foot model of the *Golden Falcon*'s got to sit on a table anyhow, but we could work it out so all the other Sinnett Harbor ships are right at eye level."

Satisfied with that arrangement, they set to work

carefully, sorting the models by dates and types. Then Tim climbed up on a stepladder and Judy handed them up to him, one by one. They were giving a superb eighteen-inch model of Bold Dick's *Sea Hawk* the center place of honor when Mr. Teed strolled back into the browsing room. "I see I slipped up on my job," he commented. But to Judy's relief, he seemed content to let it go at that and stand idle as she and Tim continued their teamwork.

"You know Ranger Wade, don't you, Mr. Teed?" she asked, and the writer nodded.

"He settled me in my cabin yesterday when I moved over to the Park," he said cheerfully. "I really didn't intend to desert you, Miss Carrington, but I finished my assignment and saw that framed plan of the wing on the wall over there; so I strolled off on a tour of inspection. Sand Winter certainly went to town here," he added admiringly. "In fact, I was tempted to talk a chapter into a dictating machine in one of those workshops just to stake out a claim!"

"Then I'm glad you were strong-minded enough to resist," Judy admitted. "Those workshops aren't open yet. Even Mr. Winter won't move into his until Monday. Dedicating this wing's supposed to be the starting gun for the whole Bold Dick celebration."

"Far be it from me to jump any guns," Glen Teed said hastily. "Meanwhile, I'll make a suggestion for what it's worth: locks on those workshop doors. I'm surprised Winter didn't think of it, if only to protect the library from possibly unpleasant accusations of losing manuscripts."

"But we simply couldn't have locks," Judy protested. "The cleaning women have to come in before we open. I don't see how anything could get lost anyway, unless an author is careless enough to leave material on his desk. Those offices all have filing cabinets with Yale locks, and that's a big concession in this town! Besides, even if a man forgot to lock his cabinet, no cleaning woman is ever going to go snooping into a drawer to dust."

"Fortunately you're right," Mr. Teed said, laughing, "because if I know authors, we're all going to forget to lock those drawers. What's worse, we'd probably lose the keys if we did."

Tim set the last model in place and waited for critical comments. "Speak now or forever after hold your peace," he warned them as he poised on the top of the ladder.

"They look exceedingly effective to me," Mr. Teed said, and Judy agreed with him wholeheartedly.

"Let's lock up then and go reward me with a lobster roll," Tim said, jumping down. "You care to join us, sir?"

The writer, however, was looking at his watch. "I have a better idea," he suggested. "Barry St. Leger's doing the last act of *The Lady and the Pirate* tonight. How about coming over to the theater with me to watch rehearsal?"

71

## 9 · Show and Shadow

To the three from the empty library,
the summer theater seemed about
ready to explode with sound and fury when they ambled
down the center aisle. In the orchestra pit the brasses
were having a field day; center stage a lusty chorus of
Bold Dick's pirates was hornpiping at the foot of the
gallows, and from the gangplank of the *Sea Hawk*, Barry
St. Leger, his hair tousled and his shirttails flapping, was
wigwagging violently at Sam Runner, perched cross-
legged on top of the piano.

Judy eyed the playwright, entranced. "Does he always park on pianos at rehearsal?" she asked.

"Generally he's sprawled on the back of his neck in
the front row," Glen Teed told her. "When he starts
climbing, he's trouble-shooting. St. Leger must want
something revamped."

"But the show starts Monday," Judy exclaimed.
"How can he change anything at this late date?"

"He'll be making changes straight through dress rehearsal," Mr. Teed said drily. "Believe me, I know! I

72

was in his company for three summers before I quit acting for newspaper work."

Judy stared at him in astonishment, but Tim suddenly chuckled. "Now I know why you made the rest of them look like hams on that TV show last April," he said. "I kept wondering whether it was just because you'd written the play, or whether you really had a flair for acting. Didn't you see it, Judy?" But she shook her head, and he went on to explain. "It was a murder show acted by a bunch of mystery writers. Mr. Teed's yarn had all their detectives tangled up in a murder and a fire at a hospital, and each one played his own man. They had such a good time, you couldn't help getting a bang out of them, but except for Mr. Teed's, the acting was strictly for the birds."

Their host looked pleased with the compliment, but he waved a deprecating hand. "Third-rate," he said. "That's all I ever would have been and I finally had sense enough to see it. You can't work with St. Leger, though, without learning something. There's nobody in the business who knows better what he's doing."

"Well, you could write a book on what I don't know about producing," Tim said cheerfully, "but if that guy has to get a show for Monday out of the chaos on this stage now, he *needs* to know what he's doing. I'm beginning to be glad we've got tickets for the last performance!"

But when he telephoned Judy at the library next morning, their Saturday-night seats were nothing in his life.

73

"Get your top hat out of hock and wash behind your ears," he ordered jubilantly. "Mr. Winter just blew over with tickets for us for opening night. Front row, Judy, right next to his. If you're on duty, for the love of Mike, get busy and do things about it."

"I'll switch with somebody," Judy promised happily. "I know I can. Nobody else is going Monday night anyway, except Miss Leonard. And if Mr. Winter wants any more prowlers tackled, just tell him it'll be a pleasure!"

"You'd better apply for your license as a private eye," Tim assured her. "I've already signed us on as permanent shadow-chasers. I won't see you tomorrow, worse luck; I'm on till midnight. So I'll pick you up about eight on Monday. Be ready, can you? We want to see the celebrities stroll in."

On Saturday morning nothing could have sounded simpler. By one-thirty Monday, however, Judy doubted whether she would survive to see *any* performance of *The Lady and the Pirate,* much less be ready and in her right mind at eight o'clock that night. What seemed like the entire population of the state of Maine was already jammed on the Mall to watch Sinnett Harbor's dignitaries, in full colonial costume, assemble for the dedication of the library wing, and people still kept turning in off Ship Street.

"Look quick. Here come Miss Leonard and Captain Matt!" Their young page's excited elbow banged into Judy's ribs from her ringside seat at a front window. "Isn't the captain a riot in that wig? No jest, Judy, I

74

never saw so many people in Sinnett Harbor before in my life!"

"No jest!" Judy agreed fervently. If even a quarter of that mob tried to crowd in for the library's open house after the dedication, the place was going to be sheer bedlam.

Luckily for the staff, though, the weather was perfect, and the last words of the speeches had no more than died away before the majority of the crowd began to drift, chattering and laughing, toward the special buses running to Gun Point Park, where they could swim and picnic or be ferried out to climb aboard the old wooden ships in Bold Dick's Anchorage. But even at that there were still six or seven hundred people to be organized into groups small enough for staff or board members to handle on guided tours and three times that many questions to be answered. What's more, Captain Matt's models and the library's collection of modern manuscripts and original jacket designs invariably made each group lose any time sense it had had in the beginning.

"Maybe the board could dream up a rule against breathing on those things," Judy told Mr. Winter and Captain Matt when the last people still showed no sign of leaving at five-forty-five. "You know, like rare-book collections have to protect their illuminated medieval manuscripts. That's about the only way we'll ever get them out of here!"

Eventually, though, the last group did clatter down the front path, and a weary board promptly declared a night's holiday.

75

"If the staff's feet feel like mine," Sandys Winter said plaintively, "there isn't a soul in town who can't wait till tomorrow to use this library. Hang a 'closed' sign on the door, and let's all go buy some arch supporters!"

But Judy had other ideas, and she tore into a bathing suit as soon as she got back to her room at the Dunnings.

"I promise not to be late for that late supper," she said when she poked her head in the kitchen to find Captain and Mrs. Matt, "but I can't think of any faster way to shrink my feet back to high-heel size than to jump off your float."

"I guess I won't fret any about your lingering," Jen Dunning said comfortably. "I'm more likely to have to send Matt along to play St. Bernard." The little laugh lines around her eyes deepened. "Maybelle Gillen claims Peleg frostbit two fingers just getting the lobsters out of his pound for our stew."

At supper, however, Judy was feeling wonderful. "The treatment may have been heroic," she told them, "but at least it worked. I'm practically a new woman —only I'm just as glad this stew is good and hot."

And in spite of rushing madly, she was still feeling like a new woman when Tim finally managed to find a parking spot and they strolled down the theater aisle to their seats. If you have to look tailored in a library every day, she thought contentedly, an evening dress and an unexpected orchid do things for your morale. Besides, a white dinner jacket instead of a uniform was no disadvantage to Tim's dark hair and deep tan, and admiring feminine glances at her escort never hurt any girl's morale either.

All around them, people settling into their seats were speculating enthusiastically about the show. The opening night of a Runner and Harne musical was event enough to have brought critics and theatrical people from considerable distances, and Judy's eyes widened when she caught three names a little way behind them.

"One star, one columnist, and one theater critic from New York anyway," she murmured to Tim. "No wonder those men in the lobby seemed so sure *The Lady and the Pirate* would be opening on Broadway later."

"There are a couple of Boston newspaper critics across the aisle, too," he told her. "Over there just beyond Miss Leonard and Captain and Mrs. Matt. They turned up in the Park this afternoon wanting a cabin, but they might just as well have asked for the Koh-i-noor diamond. The Chief even tried to get your friend Mr. Teed to let them share his, but he wasn't having one of his attacks of altruism. First come, first served was his motto. We finally set up army cots for them in the Ranger Station."

"If you hadn't, they'd be commuting to Dyer's Cove or Cranberry Horn," Judy said. "This town's jam-packed." She glanced up the aisle again and turned excitedly back to Tim. "Here comes Mr. Winter now, and he's got Mr. Runner and Mr. Harne with him. It must be nearly curtain time. I wonder if they're nervous."

"After that rehearsal Friday night, they ought to be chewing their fingernails," Tim said bluntly.

But the three who slipped into the seats beside them seemed in high spirits. "Keep your fingers crossed," Sam Runner said, smiling. "Here we go."

Then the lights dimmed and the curtain rose to a rollicking sea chantey. The show was on, and from that opening chorus of Bold Dick's freebooters to the last love song in the shadow of the gallows on Gibbet Ridge, it swept an exuberant audience with it. At intermission half the theater was already humming the new Runner tunes, and when the final curtain rang down, the roar of applause brought the playwrights and Sandys Winter, as well as the cast and Barry St. Leger, onto the stage again and again and again.

"I'd have sworn it would be a mess," Tim exclaimed, clapping doggedly.

"So would I," Judy admitted, "and now here I am with blisters on my hands. I hate to have the evening end. Sitting in all this reflected glory is probably the closest I'll ever get to being a celebrity!"

Nobody connected with the show, however, had any intention of letting the evening die so young. Almost before they knew what was happening, Judy and Tim found themselves being propelled on stage by a pair of triumphant playwrights. Sandys Winter was telephoning the Whistling Clam. Sandwiches and coffee were on the way, and celebration was in order. In fact, the celebration went merrily on till the town clock struck one and Barry St. Leger began to make disconcerting remarks about a rehearsal at nine-thirty.

"The whole evening was terrific. We can't even begin to thank you," Judy told Mr. Winter when they finally wandered reluctantly out the door, and Tim added hearty agreement.

"By the way, can I give you a lift back to the Ridge, sir?" he asked.

But the novelist shook his head. "Not this time, thanks. My car's just back of the building."

"That's more than mine is," Tim said cheerfully. "Come on, Judy. We'd better start hiking. Good night, Mr. Winter, and thanks again."

Somehow, though, with the night star-spangled and the breeze gloriously salt, prosaic working hours still seemed a long way off, and they wandered along Ship Street without a care.

"We can always worry about alarm clocks after they go off," Judy said nonchalantly.

For the moment she had forgotten that Tim had parked near the library, but she began to laugh when the building loomed over her.

"Nemesis," she said, wrinkling her nose. "Maybe I'd better start remembering that alarm after all."

She glanced idly up at the reflection of the street lights in a nearby window while Tim unlocked the car. The ghost of Bold Dick burning the midnight oil, she thought with amusement. I knew he'd walk before the summer ended. Then she gave a little gasp of surprise.

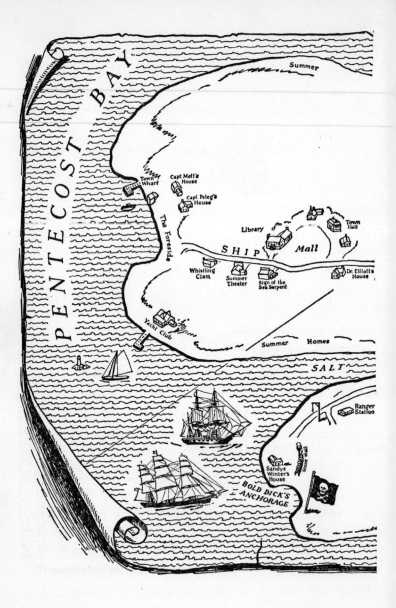

PENTECOST BAY

Summer

Town Wharf

Capt. Matt's House

Capt. Peleg's House

Library

Town Hall

S H I P   Mall

Whistling Clam

Summer Theater

Sign of the Sea Serpent

Dr. Elliott's House

The Foreside

Yacht Club

Summer Homes

SALT

Ranger Station

Sandy Winter's House

Stone Wall

BOLD DICK'S ANCHORAGE

Homes

TO DYER'S COVE

STREET

INLET

GALLOWS ROAD

GUN POINT

NATIONAL PARK

Bold Dick

Cub Campsite

BREAKFAST COVE

Map of
SiNNETT
HARBOR

"Why, there's a moving light inside the library. How queer."

At the bewilderment in her voice, Tim turned around and stared. "Somebody with a flashlight," he told her, "and a sizable one by its beam. Probably your night watchman, Judy."

"We haven't got one," she protested. "Of course, the staff all have keys, but what would any of us be doing in there at this hour? We don't love work *that* much!"

"Who else has a key?" Tim asked.

"Only Captain Matt as chairman of the board," she said promptly, "and don't try to convince me he's in there now, Tim Wade. He gets up with the birds." Judy bit her lip, looking worried. "It's his models that bother me—those and the manuscripts. Some of the people hanging around them this afternoon were plain weird. And I haven't even got my key! What under the sun should we do?"

"Get in the same way the other fellow did," Tim said practically. "He probably used a window around back. It's a cinch he didn't try this side where the street lights are."

They hurried past the end of the building and began to pick their way cautiously in the dark.

"Watch it, Judy," Tim warned her. "Stand still a minute till I see what we're up against. I just stumbled into something."

Freezing dutifully, Judy heard him grope along the bricks and then give a grunt of satisfaction.

"We've struck pay dirt," he exclaimed. "There are a

82

couple of boxes piled up here. The gent with the flash-light must have thought there was 'welcome' on your mat."

"Well, there wasn't," she said indignantly. "These boxes weren't even in sight. Miss Leonard made the workmen stow all their junk before the dedication. I watched them put everything behind the lilac hedge myself."

"Sounds as if he came with malice aforethought all right," Tim conceded. Stepping up on the boxes, he felt for the window and whistled softly. "Thoughtful sort of a guy," he said. "He didn't bother to shut it behind him. Maybe he found it open. You think this window was locked, Judy?"

"Why, it must have been," she told him. "Mr. Teed said he'd close it for me, and he's so methodical he probably checked it off on a list."

Grunting assent, Tim vaulted inside and reached out to help Judy through. "Where the deuce are we anyway?" he whispered. "I've lost my bearings."

"In the stacks at the back of the reference room, but that light was moving toward the new wing." Judy's voice was just audible. "Should I get us a flash or turn on the lights or what?"

"I've got a pencil flash in my pocket. That's plenty for now." Tim turned the tiny beam on the floor and pulled her quickly after him. "Only when we do need lights, you'll have to take care of them, Judy. I don't know where anything grows in this place."

From the wing ahead of them oddments of sound

83

were beginning to float back, and they stopped for a second outside the new browsing room to listen. "Not in there," Judy murmured. "He's farther along, Tim."

Then in the blackness beyond came a muffled crash, and Tim started to run. "Lights, quick, Judy," he begged, and she jumped for the switch, stumbling after him across the room, both of them half-blinded in the sudden light.

"He's cornered, Tim," she panted. "He's in one of the workshops and the hallway's a dead end. The door isn't even hung yet."

Fumbling around the doorframe, she found another switch, and Tim rocketed down the hall. "The last office, Judy," he shouted. "The door's closed."

When she caught up with him, though, he was running into the office next to that one and she tore in at his heels.

"Chair wedged under the doorknob, but I heard him at the window," he said briefly as he shoved the casement open and swung onto the sill. "There's still a chance I can nab him before he drops."

But Judy's fingers were digging into his shoulder. "Do you see it?" she whispered. "Down there by the birches—where our light streams out. The twisted shadow!"

## 10 · *Package for Sandys Winter*

S URE, it was twisted," Tim said, "but
there's no use getting clutched about
it. Any shadow'd twist in this breeze. Look at the ones
the branches are making."

But Judy stuck to her point. "This one was twisted
before the wind got at it," she insisted. "Honestly,
Tim. I know it sounds crazy, but whoever made this
one was scuttling along, all scrunched up just like that
faceless man on Gibbet Ridge."

Tim jumped back to the floor beside her, looking
thoughtful. "Actually there's not a thing against its
being the same man," he admitted. "Just because we
thought he'd left town doesn't mean he did. Anyway,
you got a much better look both times than I did, Judy."
He closed the window behind him and headed her for
the door. "A thief's a thief. Maybe he just saw that
stuff sitting pretty here this afternoon and thought it
was time to get busy again. I guess we'd better check
the browsing room. There couldn't be anything he'd
want in these offices, could there?"

"Not unless he felt strong enough to lug off some dictating machines," Judy told him. "Nobody's even used—" Her sentence suddenly trailed off and she darted for the hall, towing Tim after her. "I always knew I'd end up with senile decay!" she exclaimed. "My goodness, Tim, Mr. Winter moved into that end office this morning!"

The wedged door still refused to budge, however, no matter what they did, and Tim grew tired of the struggle. "Never mind," he said. "I can climb from one window sill to the other. At least that guy left something open."

Waiting impatiently in the hall, Judy finally heard the scrape of his feet against Mr. Winter's window ledge. Then a gleam of light showed at the top of the door, and he yanked the chair out from under the knob to let her in. "There's our crash," he said, pointing at a sectional bookcase and the volumes of an encyclopedia in a jumble on the floor. "I nearly broke my neck over that pile before I found the light switch."

But Judy was too busy looking at the desk to bother about an empty bookcase. "Why, he even snooped at the mail," she said in astonishment. "Those parcel-post packages were on top of the filing cabinet. I know because Mr. Winter brought them over from the Ridge this morning and he called me in here to show me where he'd put them. I'm supposed to give them to Captain Matt when he comes for them. They're some stuff for repairs on the *Ellen*."

"You don't think Mr. Winter moved them himself

later?" Tim asked, and she shook her head vigorously. "We left the room together, Tim. He was in a rush to get home to eat and change into his Bold Dick costume."

She frowned at the scattered volumes of the encyclopedia and the open drawers of the filing cabinet and the desk. "I hate to have Mr. Winter walk in on this mess. He's meticulously neat. Do you suppose we'd be destroying evidence if we just picked up the books and shut the drawers?"

Tim grinned broadly. "Who's coming to look for any?" he inquired. "The constable went out with the herring fleet last Monday. After all, Mr. Winter will know whether anything is missing, and straightening up won't interfere with that." Moving back across the room, he started restacking the sections of the bookcase while Judy tackled the cabinet and the desk, checking the contents of the drawers as she closed them, gathering scattered paper clips, and replacing the parcels for Captain Matt where they belonged.

"You know, Tim, I don't think *anything* is missing," she announced at last. "The file hasn't even been used yet, and the desk's filled with carbon and typewriter paper. I don't see how another thing could have been got into these drawers. They're full to the brim now."

"Frankly I don't think anything is missing either," Tim told her. He put the last volume of the encyclopedia on its shelf and sat back on his heels to look at her. "Could you visualize this room the way it was when you came in this morning? Try and think, Judy. Was there any kind of box or carton around—maybe something that Mr. Winter hadn't had a chance to unpack?"

Judy stayed silent a minute, trying to concentrate. Then she shook her head slowly. "I don't think so," she said. "It was the orderliness of the room that impressed me. When somebody's moving in, you expect to see boxes parked on chairs and desks, but there wasn't a thing like that. All I remember, beside those packages for Captain Matt, is the notebook Mr. Winter had in his hand—just an ordinary five-and-dime one. He put it in the top desk drawer and it's still there. No pages torn out even. I checked."

"Nothing personal at all then?" Tim said, and she shook her head again.

"Not as far as I know—except those sea-gull bookends. Maybe that's the reason I noticed them. Why, Tim?"

"Because whoever engineered this search must have been hunting for something he figured Mr. Winter was likely to bring along with him. Otherwise it wouldn't make sense to ransack a man's office practically the minute he moved in."

"You mean you think it's the same man, too, don't you?" Judy asked. "So if he didn't find what he was looking for this time either, he'll try again. Is that it, Tim?"

"That's about it," Tim agreed. "Goodness knows why he didn't retackle the house on the Ridge after we quit patrolling. Maybe because he knew Mr. Winter was still on deck. Probably he'd rather risk Elvira Snow. She's getting deaf as a snake."

He snapped the lights out in Mr. Winter's workshop, and grabbed Judy's arm. "The browsing room," he exclaimed. "That ought to settle this for us. Just let me close that window in the next office and we'll take a look. If anything's missing from your exhibits, then that's the stuff this bird was really after, and we're both crazy as coots."

But the browsing room certainly produced no evidence to make them doubt their sanity. None of Captain Matt's models had been disturbed. Not even a page of a manuscript was ruffled, and they locked the building behind them to climb soberly into the Park Ford.

"Now I suppose we have to break this to Mr. Winter," Judy said unhappily, and Tim hesitated.

"Right now I can't think of a way around it," he admitted reluctantly. "But I'd like to bet that if we hadn't scared the daylights out of that guy, he'd have tidied that room himself and nobody'd have been the wiser. If he'd left a couple of things out of place on the desk, Mr. Winter would just have blamed that on the cleaning women. I can't see this cagey customer getting you people at the library on the alert when he wanted to try again. He likes privacy too much."

"Well, cagey or not, he got fooled this time," Judy said with satisfaction, "and at least we don't have to tell Mr. Winter now. Anyway, that's up to Captain Matt and the Chief Ranger to decide. Maybe the whole business will seem silly to them in broad daylight." She shivered a little, though, remembering the twisted shadowy shape under the birches. "Just the same, Captain Matt's in for a surprise tomorrow morning. For once he's going to come downstairs and find his front door locked!"

The captain and the Chief Ranger took the matter seriously enough, however, to suit even Judy. The captain's hasty phone call to Miss Leonard got Judy the morning off, and she drove to the Ranger Station with him to go over the whole story, step by step, with Tim while the two older men listened and asked questions. After that, both of them got busy on the telephone. Captain Matt found a husky young friend of his, just through with his hitch in the Marines, to act as night watchman at the library, and the Chief Ranger hastily borrowed a couple of men from Acadia National Park.

"They'll be here tonight," he said when he hung up. "That'll take care of our end comfortably. With six, we can patrol that Ridge as long as we have to, and if anyone asks questions about our increased staff, the influx of tourists will account for it. We don't want to scare our man away. We want him to drop in again, and I think Wade's right: this fellow isn't keen on taking chances. That ought to mean we can expect him when Sandys Winter goes cruising after this Bold Dick celebration ends."

"Then we don't even have to tell Mr. Winter now, do we?" Judy asked hopefully. "Maybe it'll be all over before he gets back and he won't have the strain of waiting for the blow to fall. Only, of course, he wouldn't worry about the strain on himself. He'd be in too much of a tailspin over the trouble this might cause somebody else! A lot of good that would do his heart."

"You're dead right, Judy," Captain Matt said decisively. "He'd want to stick around and see this business through to a finish. Unless something does turn up missing in that office and we can't help ourselves, I say we sail this course with our mouths shut. He's supposed to float on an even keel, and Doctor Elliot blistered my hide last week for letting him work up a head of steam over a leak on the *Flying Nancy*." Captain Matt banged an irate fist on the arm of his chair. "It'd be a sight simpler to handle a routine robbery than all this hanky-panky, though," he growled. "I wish that ugly sculpin had just made off with a few of my ship models."

"Great Scott, I don't," the Chief Ranger retorted, his eyes twinkling. "There wouldn't be any way of keeping *you* out of the picture, and I'd hate to have to cope with your blood pressure!

"Ranger Wade will keep in close touch with you, Miss Carrington," he added, turning to Judy. "It certainly seems improbable that this fellow found what he was after, but if Sandys Winter does report a loss, I want to know it promptly. These men from Acadia can't be kept longer than necessary. No Chief has any superfluous rangers to farm out to his friends."

But it was close to the end of the week before Judy had a report to give anybody. Sandys Winter had not appeared in the library again until Wednesday morning and even then he had not gone near his own workshop. Glen Teed was just moving into one, lugging a light microfilm reader with him, and the two of them spent the rest of the morning setting it up and scanning a spool of testimony from an old murder trial. Judy worked her imagination overtime inventing errands down the back hall of the new wing, but she might as well have spared the crepe rubber on her loafers. The two men left together at lunchtime, and the mystery writer was alone when he finally showed up later. Just before noon on Thursday, though, she played into luck. Then, literally bumping into Mr. Winter in the doorway of his own office, she stopped to explain she wanted the packages on top of the filing cabinet for Captain Matt.

"We couldn't have been more right either," she told the captain triumphantly a few minutes afterward. "There's absolutely nothing missing. Mr. Winter says these packages are yours with his publisher's blessing. Tarry, seagoing smells ruin his working mood, and now he'll have no excuses, nothing but a dictating machine and paper and an encyclopedia in the office!"

Watching the smile crinkling the corners of her eyes, Captain Matt threw back his head and laughed. "How noticeably did you have to sniff this caulking to get him started on that tack?" he demanded.

"Never mind," Judy said blithely. "That's some smell, but it was worth it. The Chief Ranger can hang on to those 'spares' he borrowed with a clear conscience."

"Don't worry," Captain Matt said as he turned to leave. "I'll pass the word along on my way to the *Ellen*."

And that's that, Judy thought. Mentally she could draw a line through the number one item on her week's agenda. A backlog of unfinished work from the hectic days before the dedication was stacked at her elbow now. Even one thing she could forget with impunity would be a relief.

But the trouble with the whole puzzling business in Sandys Winter's office was its refusal to stay forgotten for many hours at a stretch. The workshops were proving popular with writers from the summer colony, and every time Judy showed another one the way down that hallway, she was back in the same old groove trying to figure it out. What the intruder had thought he was going to find puzzled her most. Trying to break into a house as full of collector's items as Sandys Winter's was understandable. But ransacking his office in a public library, expecting him to have left something special intentionally lying around, seemed plain stupid to her. If Mr. Teed who only rented a Park cabin could use his office regularly every day without festooning it with his personal belongings, why on earth should Mr. Winter who had a home in town bring over something valuable for someone to steal?

Yet somehow Judy had an uncomfortable notion that their twisted shadow was not stupid, and Tim did not make her feel any more hopeful of it. "Cautious and cagey, not dumb," he argued when they got together again long enough to struggle with the pieces of the puzzle. "Probably jittery, too, now."

"If he's any worse than I am, he must shake like a

case of ague," she said dismally. "It's got so I look to see whether Mr. Winter is carrying anything that man could want before I even say 'good morning.' The last thing I ever expected was to wish Sandys Winter out of town! Now I can hardly wait to get him aboard his *Triton* and off on that cruise. Suppose something should happen to him!"

Of course, nothing will, she told herself sensibly a dozen times in the next week, not with rangers on Gibbet Ridge all night every night. Just the same, she headed the bookmobile down the library driveway Friday afternoon feeling almost giddily lighthearted for the first time in ten days. Fifteen minutes earlier the *Triton* had actually stood out of harbor with her owner at the wheel! Not even an insistent honk that made her miss her green light for Ship Street could annoy Judy at that point. She only smiled good-naturedly at Luke Estes who was blocking her exit with an express truck.

"Library might as well hang on to this," he announced cheerfully, thrusting a package from Mr. Winter's literary agents at her. No sense my traipsin' all the way down Gallows Road for nothing. Sand Winter's off cruising."

He rattled on down Ship Street, and Judy dropped the package among the books behind her. No sense my traipsing back into the building right now either, she thought, chuckling. News sure gets around this town fast.

94

## 11 · Boa in the Bananas

JUDY reached an arm out of the covers and raised the shade on the window nearest her bed.  The weather was perfect.  Bermuda shorts, she decided, and rolled lazily over again.  If I just had a penny handy, she thought, I'd flip it: heads, stay where I am; tails, get up for breakfast.  Lacking the penny, however, she sniffed at the smells drifting up the stairs, and promptly dashed for the shower.  Mrs. Matt was making cinnamon doughnuts.  After all, a day off was a day off, and she might as well do things with it.  Miss Leonard had apparently had to struggle to get it for her.  From all accounts, Captain Peleg was still shocked to the marrow of his library budget over her insistence on a holiday for each member of the staff in rotation as soon as the Bold Dick celebration ended.

The Dunnings, though, beamed approval when she joined them at the breakfast table looking ready for almost anything except a hard day's work.

"High time you got some sun on you again," Captain

Matt said decidedly. "You're beginning to bleach like a weevil in a biscuit. They're unloading a couple of produce ships across the road at the wharf this morning. You'd better go catch yourself another tan and watch somebody else hustle for a spell. It ought to be kind of refreshing."

"The idea's irresistible," Judy admitted, laughing. "This is my lazy day. I haven't even got a single plan."

But if she had none, Tim already had plenty and he was on the phone before she could finish her last doughnut.

"How come the escape from the chain gang?" Judy asked in surprise. "This early you should be busting rock."

"That stuff's strictly for the muscle boys," Tim assured her. "I draw the tough, mental assignments. 'Keep in close touch with Miss Carrington.' Remember?"

"As of now you can count on the assignment getting a whole lot tougher," she promised, and Tim chuckled.

"I know it's late to come up with anything," he said, "but you've filed off the ball and chain so I took a chance. The Chief just elected me to help Dr. Merrill. He and his towhead are throwing a clambake for the current crop of cubs. The Doctor says to tell you you're invited. How about it? Want to come?"

"It'll serve you right if I say 'yes,' " Judy told him. "When?"

"Noon," he said, "but I'll be over as soon as I get their fire going. About an hour or an hour and a half from now. Okay?"

"Okay," she echoed contentedly. "Pick me up at the wharf, though, will you, Tim, and I'll sun-bake till you show."

But all Judy's favorite sun-baking spots were pre-empted by string beans and cabbages from the two produce ships long before she strolled across the Foreside, and she finally settled on a stack of fish nets at one side. Any ultraviolet rays straying that close to the freight shed seemed likely to concentrate on her left instep, but if her shins had to argue with many more bushel baskets on a hunt for a better place, they wouldn't last long enough to acquire a tan anyway. She had not seen this much stuff piled up on the wharf since the herring fleet outfitted. Each of the independent markets in town had a couple of men on hand loading trucks, but with the ships riding high on a flood tide, crates nudged each other down the steep pitch of the gangplanks faster than they could be checked off consignments.

The Red and White Store truck nearest her, though, seemed to have beaten the rest to a draw. It looked loaded to capacity already, and Judy watched, fasci-nated, as the driver went nonchalantly on piling barrels and crates skyward. She could practically see the whole works rolling up Ship Street scattering potential New England boiled dinners, like roses, at the feet of Sinnett Harbor's housewives. What she did not foresee, how-ever, was a four-foot hamper bouncing out the minute the truck started and catapulting bunches of bananas all over her.

At her startled yelp, half a dozen men rushed in her direction, shouting after the truck, and the frightened driver jammed on his brakes to run frantically back, convinced he had knocked her down.

"Don't worry. You didn't," Judy consoled him. "I've been parked on these nets for the last hour. You just couldn't see me over those crates you were loading. But am I glad this one wasn't full of eggs!"

She struggled to her feet, clutching an armful of bananas and watched one of the men right the upended hamper. "Are the rest of them ruined?" she asked.

"Didn't improve 'em noticeably," he admitted. Tugging out a battered stalk of bananas, he was starting to hold it up for exhibit A when he dropped it back like a nest of hornets. "Snake!" he yelled and sprinted for his truck. "Everybody keep away till I get a spanner to kill it!"

Judy stared after him in astonishment. A spanner no less. What did he expect the snake to do? Sit there and wait for him to come back and whack it? He could at least have slammed down the lid! Darting indignantly forward, she kicked the hamper shut herself and stood on top of it. Tim would probably want the snake anyway and he'd be along in a minute. She'd stay right where she was till he came.

She had to listen to heated discussion about it, however. If a ranger was on the way, that was fine with everybody. None of the truck drivers felt inclined to challenge his right to reopen that hamper. But the snake hissed like a steam leak every time Judy shifted her weight, and some of them argued strenuously against allowing her to hover like Pandora over a box full of trouble. Luckily for Judy's resolution, Tim turned onto the wharf before the cons won the day, and she beckoned wildly at him to hurry.

"Snake," she explained when he panted up. "In the bananas, Tim. I'm standing on it."

"Not my fault she wasn't bitten either," the Red and White truck driver said uncomfortably. "That hamper slid off my load and dumped bananas all over her. Just luck the snake wasn't on those. Les Chipman found it later on a bunch inside. He was going to kill it, but the young lady wanted us to wait for you. Seems reasonable it's poison, though, seeing how those things get shipped out of Honduras."

"Could be," Tim said briefly. "At any rate, I'm glad it didn't land on Miss Carrington." He kicked a stave off an empty nail keg standing near the freight shed and cut a notch in one end of it with his knife. "Pin a snake down just back of the head with a forked stick and he can't do much harm to anyone," he said in answer to their curious questions. "If it were chilly, we could count on this fellow being pretty sluggish, but not in this warm sun. Besides, it's been a long time between meals. He's probably in good fighting trim."

"He hissed—if that means anything," Judy offered helpfully, and Tim grinned at her.

"With you cakewalking on top of me, I would, too," he said. "Hop down, Judy, and let me have a look at him."

At least Tim did not have to beg for elbowroom. Judy's hasty departure from the hamper had produced the longest, sharpest hiss yet, and when he began to raise the lid cautiously with the end of his barrel stave, the space around him had increased by a good six feet. Standing on the side lines as close as she dared to get, Judy listened in alarm when the hissing began again. This time the safety valve on the steam pipe had blown clear off! Then the snake's head darted out in a lightning strike at the barrel stave, and she smothered a gasp. Tim's left hand had suddenly shot forward, his fingers aimed just behind that angry head.

"It's a young boa constrictor," he reported cheerfully as he lifted the snake out of the fruit. "About as dangerous as a kitten." He held the reptile up for their inspection, measuring it with his eye. "This one's not much more than a baby at that. Thirty-five inches at the outside and they're eighteen when they're born. Maybe eight or nine months old."

Les Chipman slipped his spanner into his hip pocket and stared at Tim, incredulous. "How big do you calculate that thing's aiming to get before it votes?" he demanded, and at Tim's prompt "fifteen feet" he nodded. "Thought likely," he said drily. "I'll stick to the kitten. It only grows into a cat."

By the time she finally got to Gun Point Park, Judy thoroughly agreed with Les Chipman. The Red and White driver had obligingly dumped a bushel basket of brussels sprouts into paper bags to provide a traveling compartment for the boa, and he rode to the Ranger Station beside her on the front seat. Judy definitely did not trust the lid, but on the whole, she preferred a basket of boa constrictor where she could keep it under surveillance to wondering when it would topple off the back seat and release its contents. "Constrictor Constrictor Imperator," Tim called it, and the snake seemed to think it had to live up to that "imperator." "Ouch, all Gaul is being divided into three parts," she exclaimed when it struck at the side of the basket nearest her arm. "Hail, Caesar! Julius and Junior, Tim Wade! What a combination!"

Judy did not shed any tears over her loss, either, when Tim left Caesar behind them at the Ranger Station, properly caged and fed. Even if she were denied the privilege of playing nursemaid to another snake for the rest of the day, she had a strong conviction that she could control her sorrow. About now the thing she felt most competent to take care of was a large Maine lobster steamed in seaweed over a clambake fire, and she wrinkled her nose appreciatively at the smell of hot, wet rockweed when they drove into Breakfast Cove.

"Look, the ranger's got the bookmobile lady," Jimmy Merrill shouted, and the pair of them were hustled down to the beach by a whooping gang of small boys.

"How come you were so slow getting back here?" Jimmy asked when the three began building a fireplace for the coffee pot. "Couldn't you find Miss Judy?"

"Finding her was the easy part," Tim said solemnly, "but she wouldn't get in the car until I could find a boa constrictor to ride with her. Boy, was that a toughie! I thought we'd never get here. Then, what do you know? It turned out she was standing right on top of one!"

Jimmy's grin threatened to lift off the top of his head.

"Broth—errr, you sure can tell 'em," he said admiringly, and Tim grinned back at him.

"There's more truth than poetry in that yarn, though, Jimmy," he told the boy. "We really did bring a baby boa constrictor over to the Ranger Station. You can come see him tomorrow if you like. He'd traveled all the way from Honduras in a hamper of bananas. One of the truck drivers down at the wharf found him, but if Miss Judy hadn't kicked the lid of the hamper shut and stood on it till I got there, he'd have crawled right out and been killed sure as shooting."

"Jeepers," Jimmy said, awed. "A boa constrictor! You bet I'll be over." He scrambled to his feet, his eyes shining. "I'll be straight back," he assured them. "I just want to go tell Dad. Golly, he thinks Miss Judy's swell, but I bet he didn't think she had this much sense!"

He streaked across to the bake fire, shouting excitedly at Dr. Merrill, and Judy laughed till she nearly dropped the coffee pot. "Here, take it," she gasped. "Oh dear, that was the most beautiful backhanded compliment I ever heard in my life."

Watching her shaking shoulders, Tim rescued the coffee pot in a hurry and peered owlishly into the spout. "Cross my palm with silver, lady," he begged. "These tea leaves say you've just acquired a towheaded admirer. A 'beautiful backhanded compliment' says she! Humph. I'm glad that kid's nine instead of twenty."

## 12 · *Lights on the* Ellen B.

TO Judy's consternation, basking in Jimmy Merrill's good graces turned out to be no mere passive state, and instead of lying on her stomach restfully digesting lobster, she spent the afternoon sweating it out on the baseball diamond.

"I'll never speak to Caesar again," she panted at Tim as she skidded safely past him to first base. "Look what he got me into!"

But Tim was as hot and disheveled as she was by the time the game ended, and it took no salesmanship on Jimmy's part to persuade both of them to stop at the Merrill cabin for soda when he cadged a ride while his father was playing taxi for cubs.

"Whew, even *pink* lemonade would be okay," Tim admitted as they raided the icebox, and Jimmy beamed happily.

"Let's drink till we find out whether we bubble," he suggested with experimental zeal. "Mom's gone to the store with another lady; so pretty soon she'll bring back a lot more." But he set his own bottle of grapeade down on the front step after one gulp. "Gee whiz, I just remembered. I gotta ask you somethin'," he told Tim. Bouncing up, he disappeared around the side of the cabin and came back lugging a cage. "It's this snake," he explained. "Dad says maybe it's just a kind of garter snake, but I don't think so for sure."

Tim, however, was already lifting out a small brownish snake and shaking his head. "Not a garter snake, Jimmy," he said. "A DeKay's snake. They turn up in gardens even in a city, just like the garters, but, look, they don't have three longitudinal yellowish stripes. They're just plain brown or gray. Of course, sometimes the garter snake's pattern varies, but it almost always has the two side stripes. They run along the second and third rows of scales counting up from the belly. Next time you catch one, count and see."

What a cheery idea that is, Judy thought, getting hastily on her feet. This was definitely no place for her. In about two minutes something was going to remind Jimmy of Tim's tale of her passion for boa constrictors and he'd be parking that horrible slimy thing in her lap to play with.

"We've got to be going, Jimmy," she announced firmly. "The ranger has to drive me all the way to the Foreside."

She was not destined to get off that easily, though. Jimmy was already whooping off on a garter-snake hunt. "I know where I can get one to count," he shouted. Still running, he looked back over his shoulder, stabbing excitedly at the remains of an old stone wall ahead of him along the top of the ledges, and Judy cried out in warning. "Watch it, Jimmy. You're close to the edge," she yelled. Then paralyzed, she saw him pitch headlong out of sight.

"Here, hold this snake," Tim ordered, shooting past her, and Judy's hand went out automatically. You can faint later, she told herself sternly, and began to run. Even a five-foot fall could be deadly when there were only rocks to land on! In front of her, Tim had vanished over the ledge, and she peered down, limp with relief, as she panted up. He was already starting back with Jimmy in his arms. She could hear both their voices.

"He landed on a bayberry bush halfway down," Tim called up reassuringly. "He looks as if he'd been in a cat fight, but he's all right."

Over Jimmy's squirming protests, Tim carried him to the porch and parked him against Judy's shoulder. "Now quit yaking and listen," he said firmly. "If you're going to be a herpetologist, you've got to look where you're heading. You can't just put your hands and feet down any old place. That's an important thing you can train yourself to do right now, Jimmy. It's too late to wish you had after a copperhead strikes."

Tim turned hopefully at the sound of a car and nodded with satisfaction. "Here comes your dad now to patch up your scratches," he told the youngster. "So everything's jake again. Only how do you think we can persuade Miss Judy to take off that new bracelet she's wearing and let us put it back in its cage?"

Suppressing a grin, he stared pointedly at Judy's arm

and she looked down, incredulous. She was still clutching Jimmy's snake behind its head, but the rest of its twelve inches was coiled serenely around her wrist. "Oh my goodness," she gasped. "Tim, I forgot I had it! Why, it's not slimy at all."

But slimy or not slimy, snakes were still not on Judy's list of preferred pets, and when the *Harbor Breeze* made its weekly appearance on Thursday, she took a dim view of one of its feature articles. She had been feeling like Laocoön all summer, and this full page, with pictures, about Assistant Ranger Timothy Wade struck her as unlikely to improve her lot. Tim had a one-track mind now. His interest in snakes did not need any encouragement. Let the enemy land and he'll rescue Junior first and me later—if there happens to be some time left over, she thought gloomily. Still, she could not help chuckling when she read the feature. Between the pictures and the write-up, Tim sounded like the original Hopi snake dancer. If the town did not think his room was a den of rattlesnakes, it was not the fault of the *Harbor Breeze*. At least she could dream up a lot of pertinent comments on this one to go with their shrimp cocktails in Portland Saturday night!

When Saturday rolled around, though, their plans for dinner and a show in Portland blew up in their faces. Tim got last-minute orders to pinch-hit on Gibbet Ridge for an injured ranger, and at six-thirty Judy was waiting outside the Whistling Clam in dungarees, her arms loaded with lobster rolls and coffee, instead of strolling down Congress Street in nylons.

"Think nothing of it," she told an apologetic Tim. "I'm the rugged, adventurous type. By the way, do I hide on the floor when we drive past the Ranger Station or can I put in a bill for three hours at my regular rates for patrol service?"

"You hide on the floor," Tim reported with pleasure. "The Chief was properly scandalized at the mere mention of my taking you along to the Ridge. Quote: Miss Carrington's company during your time on duty would be highly irregular, unquote. But he did say he certainly wishes you luck with the picnic you're throwing on Bold Dick Beach this evening! You'd better start turning into the mountain-goat type. We've got a heck of a lot of climbing before we hit a ledge where you can dangle your feet officially over Bold Dick's territory."

There could not be a more perfect spot, however, Judy decided when they had clambered out on the rocks —the warm scent of pines and a fabulous sunset, and down below them the Bay and the old wooden ships rocking lazily with the spank of the incoming tide. On a night like this it was utterly fantastic to remember that she was sitting here only because a ranger was watching for a twisted shadow without a face. Leaning back against the ledge, coffee cup in hand, she cast a covert glance at Tim. He was not forgetting, she noticed. For all his apparent relaxed ease his eyes kept roaming the Ridge.

"The *Triton*'s due back tomorrow," he remarked suddenly. "Our bright idea seems to have fallen flat on its face, Judy. Ten days and nothing's happened. What's the guy waiting for?"

"Maybe he reads the *Breeze*," Judy said sweetly. "He's probably practicing up on snake charming."

But Tim only grinned at her. "That's an idea," he said, unruffled. "I ought to send you legging back for my bodyguard. After all, tonight's the Shadow's last chance. The Chief's putting two men on each of the later shifts. If I hadn't been standing this early one, he'd never have winked at your being here. This guy's so cagey it's beginning to get him bothered."

"Our mystery man's not as dumb as I hoped he was," Judy admitted. "Just the same, unless he's a mind reader, he can't know you've got the Ridge patrolled. The rangers certainly haven't been obvious about it. Captain Matt and I have been over twice at night to see Elvira since Mr. Winter left and we couldn't find one anywhere. Don't think we didn't look either!"

"Well, we haven't been wearing luminous paint after dark for his benefit," Tim agreed. "We show on the Ridge the same as usual; that's all—like me loafing around picnicking on my night off." He smiled at her ruefully as he smothered the embers of their driftwood fire. It was chilly and dark without the blaze. The ledges were no longer hospitable, and they half slid, half scrambled, back to the grass by the beam of his electric torch.

"We might as well keep moving and stay warm," Tim decided, heading her along the path over the Ridge, "and we aren't going to imitate the invisible man either,

Judy. Keeping out of sight sure hasn't worked. Maybe if our pal's snooping, he'll go really slap-happy when he sees us leave. He's the boys on the yawn patrol's headache anyway. He always makes like an owl." Flashing his torch across the road into the surprised stare of a green tree frog, he chuckled. "The herps are out. Come on, Judy. We'll catch us a four-toed salamander."

They caught a two-lined one instead, however, completely circling the Ridge in the process, and Tim rummaged in the steel drum near their picnic ledge for their discarded sandwich box to put it in. "The perfect pet," he assured her. "Doesn't bark, scratch, or bite, and minds its own business. We'll stop at the Station and make it a terrarium on the way back." Focusing the flash on his watch a second, he grinned at her happily. "And that will be in precisely ten minutes! Where did you leave the rug and the thermos bottle? I might as well start collecting."

"Right over there at the foot of the ledges," she said, "but how about the lights on the *Ellen*, Tim? Do you leave them burning?"

"What lights?" Tim asked. He turned around and started toward her again, sounding puzzled. "You don't mean the riding lights, do you?"

"No, of course, I don't," Judy told him. "You'd better take a look for yourself, Tim, but I think they're in the cabin."

## 13 · Double Trouble

TIM stared down at the anchorage, whistling in surprise. "Asleep at the switch," he said. "You're sure those lights didn't just come on, Judy?"

"Dreamer!" she retorted. "They've been on at least since we got back. I saw them when you were standing on your head in the trash barrel."

"As far as we're concerned, they could have been on since dark I guess," he admitted, shrugging. "From here the *Ellen*'s been pretty well hidden behind the *Falcon* and the *Nancy*. She's just swung around with the tide." He parked the salamander's box on top of the thermos bottle and the rug he was already carrying and steered Judy along the sloping path from the Ridge to the beach. "You're going to get a nice dark row for a reward," he announced. "Only I'd sure like to know who's been out there. I'd buy him some string to tie around his finger next time."

"I'll relay the offer," Judy said, laughing, as she settled in the skiff. "At least, I take it Captain Matt's guilty. He said he was coming over after supper. Didn't he phone the Station?"

"Probably," Tim told her with resignation. "He always does so we won't think we have to go tearing out to investigate. But little bright eyes here was figuring he was off duty and didn't look at the logbook. Could be he's still out there? Maybe?"

But Judy shook her head. "Keep right on rowing," she ordered. "Captain Matt was sailing over in the *Tern* between two trips to Dyer's Cove. He had to take his wife to a social at her sister's church and go back to pick her up at nine-thirty. I know because he stopped after the library-board meeting to tell me in case I got home first. I even gave him the package the expressman had just left for Mr. Winter and he said he'd stop at the wharf and leave it with Elvira. He must just have gone on working aboard the *Ellen*, Tim, until he happened to look at his watch, and then torn off forgetting everything."

Tim nodded. "It makes sense—" he grumbled, "only if he'd forgotten and left us a slice of moon while he was at it, I'd forgive him a whole lot faster."

Once they got past the *Falcon* and the *Nancy*, however, the lights streamed out of the *Ellen*'s cabin to substitute for his slice of moon, and Tim tied the skiff to the schooner's boarding ladder in a hurry. Something about the lights still bothered him, though, even after they climbed aboard, Judy discovered. He kept frowning down at their path in the water.

"Judy, did you go home before we came over here?" he asked suddenly, and she looked at him, mystified.

"Why, no, I didn't have time enough," she told him. "Miss Leonard had to rush to the dentist and I stayed late. We weren't going to Portland so it didn't matter, but I even had to borrow these dungarees from our page in order to meet you by six-thirty. What on earth are you trying to get at now?"

"Only whether Mrs. Matt could have changed her mind without your knowing it," Tim explained. "Maybe the church social got called off. Because Captain Matt never pulled away from this schooner after dark without noticing these lights. He couldn't have. Up on the Ridge all we got was the glow inside the cabin. But look at them out here on the water. They might as well be Pound O' Tea Light." He linked her arm through his and strode energetically across the deck. "Either Captain Matt's still aboard this schooner or somebody turned the lights on again after he left. All I want to know is which."

"Well, you're about to find out," Judy assured him. She cocked her head to one side, motioning him to listen. "Hear that rustle? Somebody's inside now, Tim."

"Okay, let's knock," he said laconically, and they banged a duet on the door. "Hi," Tim shouted. "Put out the welcome mat. You've got visitors."

The answer he got, however, was a slammed door on the opposite side of the cabin, and he wrenched angrily at the knob under his hand. "The same old chair trick, Judy," he growled, "and by the time we can get around the bow, he'll be thumbing his nose at us. He must have come aboard from the seaward side."

To prove Tim's words, the roar of an outboard motor exploded in the stillness, and he listened in disgust. "The one place where no one was waiting for him," he said bitterly. "That guy's not just cagey; he plays into luck."

"The whole performance had his earmarks," Judy admitted. "It couldn't have been anybody else except the Shadow."

"Not unless breaking and entering is getting contagious around this town," Tim said with conviction. "But for the love of Mike, why pick on the *Ellen?* How many places is Mr. Winter supposed to leave his personal belongings lying around? What's this schooner got in common with his office in the library?"

"Ask me that again!" Judy exclaimed in an odd voice.

Tim blinked at her as if she had lost her wits. "Ask you what again?" he demanded.

But she was already shaking her head. "Never mind, I've got it," she said excitedly. "Express packages, Tim! That's what the Shadow could think they had in common. There were three in Mr. Winter's office that night." Her eyes widened with dismay. "Only that would mean it's someone I know," she said unbelievingly. "He'd have to have been in the library when I gave Captain Matt this one."

"For all we know he could be Miss Leonard's great-uncle," Tim pointed out promptly. "Anyway, there's no law against his using the library. You've come up with the only idea any of us has had yet, Judy. Don't try to louse it up."

Seizing her arm, he hurried her down the deck. "If you're right, this bird didn't even have to do any guessing. He tailed Captain Matt so he'd know whether the *Tern* stopped at the Winter wharf coming or going. All he had to do was raid the right place later. It still burns me, but with his luck it would be the *Ellen*."

The litter of torn wrappings on the table in the cabin did nothing to reassure either of them as they rushed in and Judy gave an ejaculation of surprised relief when Tim unearthed a bulky, weather-stained copybook among the debris.

"Why, it's an old sea captain's journal," she said, studying the spidery writing on the cover. "Mr. Winter certainly noses them out. He must have shipped it in for his collection."

"Apparently our night crawler doesn't give a hoot for Captain Jethro Bell's adventures, though," Tim remarked interestedly. "But he took the trouble to open this package, and that's more than he did for the ship chandlers' stuff in the office over at the library. If we can stay the course, Judy, we ought to get the answer by the process of elimination!"

"By now I don't care whether he wants only a three-cent stamp as long as he doesn't get it," Judy said indignantly. "If Luke Estes brings any more of Mr. Winter's express packages to the library, I'm going to sit on them till you and the Chief Ranger can come get them."

Rooting in the torn wrappings for a piece of paper

114

large enough to protect the copybook temporarily, she sent an envelope sailing to the floor and bent down mechanically to retrieve it. But she was up again in a second with a curious expression on her face.

"It's empty," she said, handing it to Tim, "but it's still stuck to a piece of gummed paper and look at the return address. Mr. Winter didn't ship this package in. It came from McIntyre and Allison, his literary agents in New York. Tim, I'm beginning to wonder!"

"Hold everything, Judy; so am I," Tim admitted. He pawed hastily through the rest of the wrappings and came up with the outside address label. "The same," he said—"in big black letters for the benefit of the U.S. Post Office and Mr. X. As of now, you quit wondering and start sitting on McIntyre and Allison packages. Mr. Allison must be buying at auctions for Mr. Winter again. Didn't he send that million-dollar log of some mutineer captain Mr. Winter showed us the last time we were over for supper? This journal must be small potatoes, but our man sure as heck wants to get his hands on something Mr. Allison's sending. We'd better get ashore, Judy, and report to the Chief."

Back at the Station, however, they did not even get out of the Ford. The Chief, it developed, had headed for town fifteen minutes earlier in response to a phone call from Captain Matt, and Tim merely dropped his salamander's box into the outstretched arms of the ranger on duty before they roared after him out Gallows Road.

"Now what the dickens has happened?" he wondered, frowning.

"Goodness only knows," Judy answered uneasily. "With this Shadow flitting around, anything I guess—though, unless he's learned to divide like an amoeba, how can he have tackled the library, too?"

But this time the library was undisturbed. It was Captain Matt's workshop that had been ransacked. Its normal shipshape order had disappeared in a clutter of gluepots and brads and pattern paper that looked as if it had been literally shoveled out of storage cupboards and dumped on his work counters, and the captain's indignation had reached a fine rolling boil.

"Make coincidence out of it if you can," he was snorting at the Chief Ranger when Tim and Judy burst in. "At least, that'd be a sight easier than trying to figure out what the same man is after in both Sand Winter's office and my workshop!"

He changed his mind, though, as he listened to Tim's report of the episode on the *Ellen*. He had rushed off late to pick up Mrs. Matt just as Judy had suspected, and until now he had not thought of the package again.

"Of all the chowder-headed performances," he flared in self-disgust. "If that sculpin had got what he wanted, I'd have only myself to blame—and a lot of good that would do Sand Winter."

"Actually you owe yourself a vote of thanks," the Chief told him. "You've brought us a step forward. We're reasonably sure what kind of thing our man's looking for. As far as I'm concerned now, the major problem is Sandys Winter. Presumably he knows what's being shipped him, and he's due in tomorrow.

How much longer have we a right to keep this business to ourselves?"

"No longer," Captain Matt said bluntly. "Sand's got to know for his own protection. But first off we'd better light a couple of firecrackers under Luke Estes. Man and boy, Luke's always been mighty solicitous of his feet, and there's no sense in Sand Winter's being waylaid some night on Gallows Road because he's toting something Luke's hired to tote."

"I can get you five volunteers from the library to light those firecrackers," Judy offered promptly. "Miss Leonard claims Luke Estes keeps cruising around the block until he can hail one of us coming back from lunch just so he can avoid walking across the driveway with a package."

"It could be our raider knows his Luke Estes," Tim said thoughtfully. "Maybe he wasn't in the library this afternoon by accident. He might figure Luke isn't likely to go all the way down Gallows Road when Mr. Winter's out of town."

" 'No use my traipsin' down Gallows Road for nothin'. Sand Winter's gone cruisin',' " Judy mimicked Luke's lazy drawl to perfection. "The *Triton* had hardly stood out of harbor before he pulled that one on me. I remember he even made me miss a green light." Suddenly her hand flew to her throat and she jumped to her feet in consternation. "There's a McIntyre and Allison package for Mr. Winter in the bookmobile," she gasped. "Luke handed it to me when I was trying to turn into Ship Street. That's what made me miss my green light."

## 14 · Storm Warnings

"AVAST, there, Judy. Luff up while we think this one over," Captain Matt ordered, and Tim pulled her back beside him, his hand reassuringly over hers.

"Stop worrying, Judy," he said firmly. "You couldn't have left that package in a safer place. It's still in the bookmobile."

"But that's what's worrying me," Judy protested. "Of course, it's still there. If anybody had messed around that bookmobile, I'd know it. Nobody else drives it, and I padlock every single door every time I put it away. Besides, the package is down behind the front seat and it's buried a foot deep under duplicates. That's why I forgot it. My goodness, Tim, all I'm worrying about is getting rid of it!"

She was so emphatic that Captain Matt chuckled. "I can't say I blame you any," he conceded, eyeing the chaos on his work counters. "It just boils down to the question of where we can put it till Sand can take charge himself."

"Leave it where it is," the Chief Ranger advised, ignoring Judy's dismayed expression. "Miss Carrington's in no danger or I wouldn't suggest it. She's been carrying that package for ten days now. Ranger Wade is right: we couldn't find a safer place for it." He turned inquiringly to Judy. "It's up to you, of course, Miss Carrington. We'll take the package in at the Ranger Station if you feel it's too much of a burden, but obviously our man has no knowledge of this one. He didn't lose much time investigating any of the others."

The Chief waved an eloquent arm at the open cupboards. "There's proof enough," he said drily. "Captain Matt didn't discover this until he and his wife came home at ten-thirty. He had rowed the package and a five-gallon can of gas out to the *Tern* before his supper so he wouldn't have to bother stopping in at the house again after his first trip to Dyer's Cove. But this search took place while he was off that first time, or the thief couldn't have been surprised aboard the *Ellen*. And you can bet your bottom dollar that the *Tern* and the captain's car would have been overhauled later if he'd brought that package back again instead of leaving it on the schooner. Why risk calling our man's attention to another one?"

"I'd better keep it," Judy admitted unhappily. "After all, what else can we do with it that'd be safe? Only now that I've remembered the thing, I know I'll act about as innocent as a cat with canary feathers sticking out of his mouth. It's a good thing Mr. Winter's coming home tomorrow."

But by Sunday noon Sandys Winter had wired Elvira from Bar Harbor that he planned to stay out six days more, and Judy faced another week of carrying the package with her on her rounds. "You might at least offer me a snake for a watchdog," she told Tim late Monday afternoon when she made her usual book-mobile stop at the Ranger Station and spotted Junior sunning himself on a rock. "Indian rajahs used cobras to guard their treasure, and what's a cobra got that Junior hasn't got?"

"Absolutely nothing except poison," Tim assured her, grinning.

Judy snapped her fingers. "Pooh," she said. "Poison went out with the Borgias. A psychological attack's the up-to-date thing, and don't try to tell me Junior isn't built for that!" She took a wary step closer to the big pine snake and pulled an egg out of a paper bag. "Jimmy Merrill sent him this, but I must say it doesn't look adequate. Will he eat it, Tim?"

"Your friend Julius Caesar would snoot it," he told her, "but Junior's in favor of eggs. Go ahead and give it to him."

Judy balked at that suggestion, however. "That's your job," she said firmly, handing him the egg. "Junior's personality still doesn't send me." Neverthe-less, she watched the feeding process with interest. "My goodness, he swallowed it whole! I can see it traveling right down his throat," she exclaimed. But suddenly the snake pressed his body against the ground, contract-ing his muscles just before and just behind the bulge, and to Judy's utter fascination, the egg shell collapsed with a distinctly discernible crunch.

"Neat?" Tim asked, and she nodded, her eyes fixed on the pine snake settling contentedly down on his rock again.

"Do all egg-eating snakes do that?" she demanded, "or is it a specialty of Junior's?"

"It's a specialty of bull snakes and their allies," Tim said, "and Junior's an eastern ally. One African snake has special cutting edges in its throat for the purpose of slicing egg shells. Then it regurgitates the fragments. But most egg eaters just swallow the egg whole and wait for the gastric juices to get busy."

"Messy and dull compared to Junior's method," Judy said with disdain. "It's all settled. I'll buy three dozen eggs for the bookmobile and invite him to slither aboard." She raised the doors along one side of the station wagon and thumbed down the shelves for the books the Ranger Station had asked for. "Look, I snatched a copy of *Midnight Means Murder* for you, and with the show opening tonight, people are practically queuing up for them. Mr. Teed's been purring all morning, but if he gets much more expansive with tickets, he won't leave a seat for himself. The last I heard he'd handed out fifty besides the ones he gave us. What's he going to do when the movie of his next book gets released?"

"We'll let him sit in our seats—at intermission when we don't need 'em," Tim said nobly. "But if you're planning to have me chase in and out of windows after *this* show, give me a ring before seven-thirty, will you, so I can wear my dungarees."

Their particular villain obligingly lay low after the performance, however, so they were able to settle for chocolate doughnuts in the Whistling Clam with half the rest of the audience instead of racing through the library after an elusive flashlight again.

"Mr. Teed certainly ought to be satisfied," Tim commented, listening to the remarks floating around them. "Everybody we've heard seems to be gung ho over his play. Anyway, he can sew up a plot for me whenever he feels like it. There wasn't a loophole in the thing."

"Glen Teed's got the kind of mind that disapproves of loopholes," Judy told him. "It's just plain methodically cautious and careful. I still can't figure out whether he writes mysteries because his mind always has worked that way or whether it works that way now because he's written so many mysteries. But, brother, is he a planner! You should see the list of instructions he gave us in case anybody telephoned or telegraphed or came looking for him when he was out of the library for lunch. So far the only thing he hasn't given us is the name of the undertaker he'd like called if he gets run over on Ship Street!"

"Cheer up; maybe he'll think of that tomorrow," Tim said.

"More likely he figures it's all right to take one calculated risk," she retorted gaily. "I suspect he'd be an awful pain in the neck to live with, but around the library he's a positive asset. I don't know how we'd manage some of the stuff Luke Estes just dumps on the doorstep if Mr. Teed didn't always show up willing to lend a hand."

Glen Teed's careful turn of mind was the last thing calculated to make Judy brood, though, and she woke up the next morning with her attention back on her own problems. At least, she was twenty-four hours safely closer to getting rid of that package, and this was not a bookmobile day. All yesterday afternoon she had felt as though she were driving a charge of dynamite around with her. But this morning, she decided firmly, she was going to shed her responsibilities and loaf in the sun, listening to Captain Peleg's scuttlebutt. After all, she did not have to report to work till one o'clock and, in Sinnett Harbor terms, it was "fairing weather."

Captain Matt was still having his regular morning session with his barometer when Judy came downstairs, but he strolled along to the dining room with her. "Show good?" he asked as they tackled Mrs. Matt's golden buckwheat cakes.

"Tops," Judy said enthusiastically. "You'd better take Mrs. Matt to see it. Tim says just watching somebody *catch* the villain for a change would be worth the price of admission. He's sure ours was sitting next to us grinning up his sleeve."

"Well, you're likely to get rid of Sandys Winter's package sooner than you expected," the captain consoled her. "Weather's making up, Judy. The barometer's falling fast. It's my guess he'll run for port."

"But it's such a beautiful day," she exclaimed in surprise. "Maybe it's just a local thunder storm brewing."

"Not this time," Captain Matt said, shaking his head.

"Storm warnings are up as far as Hatteras. Jen listened to the weather report while she was getting breakfast, and a tropical storm's two hundred miles off the coast of Florida. There'll probably be a southeast blow along the whole coast."

"Then I hope it blows Sand Winter in promptly," Mrs. Matt said with spirit. "I know you men think it's sane and sensible for Judy to hang on to that package of his, but if Alice Mariner Carrington sorts your wig when she hears of it, Matt Dunning, I won't blame her a mite."

"I can hear my leg irons clanking already," Captain Matt admitted with a twinkle. "You'd better come to my rescue, Judy. We'll take the *Tern* and go add some weight to those moorings for Sand's ships. If I keep you under my eye all morning, I might get out of the brig!"

In spite of his casual banter, however, a falling barometer caused by a tropical storm was something that Sinnett Harbor took seriously, Judy decided. Captain Peleg was already out relashing the barrels under his lobster car when the *Tern* headed for Bold Dick Anchorage, and to judge from the slabs of concrete she watched Captain Matt's winch lowering all morning, he was apparently planning to hold three ships the size of the *Queen Mary* through a howling northeaster. Stretched comfortably on the hatch of the *Tern*'s cabin, Judy followed the proceedings with lazy interest, but getting herself steamed up over the possible effects of a storm hundreds of miles away struck her as a waste of energy. Like looking under my bed every night, she thought with an inward grin.

But in a Maine coast town in the late August storm season her detached frame of mind had about as much chance as a clam in a fritter. Even at the library the remarks Judy heard oftenest for the rest of the day involved storm tides, gale winds, and last year's storm damage to lobster traps. When she strolled over to the drugstore counter for supper, it was just the same. "Doc" had his radio on and everybody in the place was absorbed in the weather reports. Consequently, when Tim blew up to the circulation desk just before noon on Friday, wearing a broad smile and looking damp around the edges, she was already conditioned.

"Rain?" she demanded. "What *is* happening outside, Tim?"

"It's souping up some. That's about all," he reported. "Just a foggy mist so far, but storm warnings are flying all the way to Eastport. People who planned to leave early next week have been pulling out of the Park this morning, figuring they might as well beat the rain, and Luke Estes says half the herring fleet's in." His smile grew broader. "In fact, you'd be surprised how much has come in."

"The *Triton!*" Judy exclaimed happily.

"About two hours ago," Tim said, nodding, "and the Chief's got everything set. Tea at four-thirty; so keep your eye peeled for a guy in uniform near the cub camp. I'll be standing there thumbing a ride."

## 15 · *Jerry Ricker's Manuscript*

JUDY spent the next hour and a half ducking Miss Leonard. The bookmobile had not missed a trip all summer, and she had no intention of letting it start breaking its record today. Not that it was actually raining, but in Miss Leonard's book "foggy mist" was probably not bookmobile weather either. Judy even ate her lunch holed up in the basement stacks finishing a reference job for the civic committee of the garden club, and by one-thirty she was streaking out the furnace-room door, the keys of the station wagon dangling in her fingers. At that, a hail from the driveway nearly gave her heart failure, but it was only Glen Teed legging after her to beg a lift to a service station.

"I left my car for a check-up this morning," he explained as they drove out Ship Street. "I just want to get it and collect some groceries before the deluge starts. With this southeast wind we might as well get set for a three-day siege." He nodded resignedly at the mist around them. "Oh well, if I get too bored, I can look out my window at rangers blotting up moisture and grow reconciled to toasting my shins again. Tramping the woods in bad weather is my idea of nothing to do."

"Maybe they'll feel the same way yet," Judy said, smiling, and Mr. Teed laughed as he climbed out.

"They'll wish they had gills I suspect," he admitted. "To quote our expressive library page, 'thanks a bundle,' Miss Carrington. I'll see you again Tuesday when the sun shines."

Probably that's the literal truth, too, Judy thought with amusement. It was hard to imagine Glen Teed bothering to struggle out in a southeaster. He was as fastidious as a cat.

Along her book route, though, people seemed to be taking the prospect of a rainy weekend in stride. In fact, as far as Judy could see, they were only waiting to pounce on her shelves for four books apiece before they holed up thoroughly happy. She even wondered whether for once her supply was going to give out completely. All summer she had averaged a circulation of four hundred volumes a week out of the five hundred the bookmobile always carried, but this Friday was breaking records. By midafternoon she was sure her eyes glittered like a miser's every time some one handed over the books a departing cabin neighbor had left for her. At least, the odds were in her favor: sixty books in from fifteen families out. With that ratio she might actually have enough science fiction left to hold Jimmy Merrill.

But temporarily, where Jimmy was concerned, science fiction had had it, and he turned down Miss Pickerell and Mars for navy hurricane hunters. "I haven't got time for spaceships," he explained. "I gotta find out about hurricanes. Did you know they name them after girls, Miss Judy? One named Carol is a thousand miles down south right now, and just the same, it's maybe going to get stormy here any minute. You ought to see the stack of logs Dad and I took inside. I bet we can keep the fire going if it rains a week!" Obviously hoping for the worst, Jimmy balanced the triple-decker mysteries his father wanted on top of his own selections, and turned on his angelic grin. "Could you bring a lot of Coast Guard rescue stories Monday, please, Miss Judy?"

"I could," Judy assured him cheerfully, "but this bookmobile isn't allowed to come out and play in the rain, Jimmy Merrill. With you in cahoots with the weatherman, something tells me I'll be sitting right in the library keeping my feet nice and dry."

And that wouldn't be such a bad deal either, she thought as she started down the road. She disliked driving in bad weather. Across the field, Tim was hurrying up from the cub camp site, and she gave him a honk.

"Did you get the kids off?" she asked, opening the door.

"They pulled out an hour ago," Tim said as he climbed in. "Whew, I'm winded. It took me longer than I thought it would to batten down that camp, and

I didn't want to keep you waiting." He piled a half-dozen books on the seat between them and smiled at her, breathless. "These are the ones the kids rounded up after you left this afternoon. I didn't see any sense leaving them there over the weekend."

"I'm glad you didn't," Judy said. "It's a help to keep my records straight as I go along, but I wasn't worrying any about them. Miss Leonard thinks its fabulous that the bookmobile's lost only fifty books this season, but she ought to give the scout camp a medal for not losing any. You wouldn't believe how long I've been chasing after Mr. Teed trying to get back just one mystery."

She swung the station wagon into the driveway on the Ridge and Tim gestured toward a man talking to Mr. Winter outside the house. "Speaking of angels," he said. "What's Mr. Teed doing out of the library at this hour? I thought he stayed till you shut up shop."

"Not when there's a southeaster hovering on the horizon," Judy said with a chuckle. "He's getting set to dig in for the duration."

She stopped beside the front porch, and the mystery writer gave them a genial salute. "This time I guarantee you've seen the last of me, Miss Carrington," he called. "I noticed the *Triton* was in so I stopped to say 'hello,' but I'm off to my lair with my loot." With a wave of his arm at the cartons of groceries piled in the back of his car, he climbed in, bumping off up the road, and Judy smiled at Sandys Winter in relief.

"You don't know how grateful we are to the weatherman," she told him: "first, for sending you home because we've missed you, and second, for luring your caller back to his cabin right now." Digging behind the front seat of the station wagon, she found the express parcel. "This is the one the Chief told you about," she explained as she and Tim followed Mr. Winter into his living room. "When I saw Mr. Teed, I was afraid we wouldn't be able to hand it over."

"Probably he would have been an asset," Mr. Winter told her with a wry smile. "Glen Teed's got an exceedingly able, logical mind. He's the man to make some sense out of this extraordinary business."

Characteristically, though, that was his last reference to the problem until he had settled his guests comfortably before the fire with a pot of coffee and a tray full of Elvira's brownies. Then picking up the package he had dropped on an end table, he tapped it thoughtfully.

"Incredible," he said at last. "I've been mulling all this over ever since the Chief Ranger and Matt Dunning stopped in this morning and I keep coming up against a blank wall."

"You don't mean you've no idea what this fellow is after, either, do you, sir?" Tim asked in astonishment.

"That's exactly what I do mean," Sandys Winter admitted. "The only two packages I've been expecting from Jack Allison are both accounted for now, and there's nothing about either of them to interest a thief. For that matter, he's already proved he didn't want my captain's journal, and this one simply contains the manuscript of a first novel by a young friend of mine who was killed in a highway accident last June. At least, I assume it's Jerry Ricker's manuscript," he amended. "I suppose I'd better check to make sure."

Reaching for a paper knife, he slit the heavy gummed tape around the package and glanced hastily at a sheaf of typewritten pages.

"That's what it is," he reported. "Jerry had sold three or four short stories, and I'm hoping his mystery will be publishable. He left an invalid mother living with relatives in Virginia. Actually, it was Jerry's land-lady who sent it along to me. She found it in his desk with my name and the McIntyre and Allison address lying on top of it when she was packing his effects." The novelist frowned down at the manuscript, shaking his head. "If Jack Allison is shipping in something special, somebody else obviously knows a lot more about it than I do!"

"Would there be any way of getting hold of him to find out?" Judy asked eagerly.

"On Sunday night there will be," Mr. Winter told her promptly. "I've already tried to reach him long distance; that's how I know. You two are hereby invited to Sunday supper. We'll call him up together the minute he gets back to New York."

"Not even a southeaster could keep us away," Judy exclaimed, and Mr. Winter smiled at her.

But his face grew grave again as he watched the fire-light flickering on the manuscript in his lap. "I'm only just beginning to realize how much my friends have spared me," he said quietly. "That Judy should have been subjected to unnecessary worry and risk over this manuscript, though, is most distressing of all. If Jack Allison hadn't just planned to bring it along when he came down for Bold Dick Week, it would have been here early in July. He finally shipped it because he had to cancel his visit."

"The trouble is that you've heard everything at once, and that made it sound much worse than it really was," Judy protested. "That man hardly got in our hair at all. Except for the wear and tear on my sense of responsibility and Captain Matt's temper, of course," she added, laughing.

"Hey, what about the wear and tear on my ego?" Tim demanded. "It got frustrated. I didn't put Sherlock Holmes out of business!"

"I'll concede that neither of you seems entirely worn out if that's what you're trying to convince me of," Mr. Winter agreed with a twinkle. "At least, I guess you still have strength enough to draw the shades. In consideration of all that wear and tear, I'll put this manuscript out of sight until I have a chance to read it next week and I'm developing an allergy to snooping."

He waited for them to finish the job. Then he led the way to the fireplace in his library. "Bold Dick's cupboard," he explained, running his hand gently over the beautiful pine paneling. "I discovered it by sheer accident when I was eighteen and Mother had set me to hard labor, waxing. But it was a long time before I succeeded in opening it again." Cupping his fingers over one of the knots in the wood, he did some acrobatic pressing with the heel of his hand and his fourth finger. "The trick is to keep your palm from touching the wood," he said as a section of the paneling swung outward, "and even now it's about all my fourth finger can do to make it. Bold Dick apparently devised the combination to fit the dimensions of his own hand and it certainly couldn't have been a ladylike one. The stuff I found hidden in here, by the way, started me on my marine collection. Charity may have reformed her pirate outwardly, but he stayed a reprobate at heart. He hung on to all the gear of his buccaneering days."

Stowing the manuscript on a shelf, he closed the panel and strolled out to the porch with Tim and Judy. "Hello, the storm's begun," he exclaimed. "Anyway, a southeaster will put a stop to our man's activities for a few days. That'll relieve my conscience. You rangers can get a night or two off, Tim. I'll see both of you again Sunday."

He turned hastily back into the house as the rain commenced to beat toward the doorway, and his guests ran for the station wagon.

"Will the rangers really quit patrolling, Tim?" Judy asked, surprised.

Tim grinned derisively. "The Chief's taken over the post office motto: 'Neither rain, snow, sleet nor hail shall stay these couriers from their appointed rounds,'" he told her. "There'll be two of us on the Ridge every night even if we have to wear swim fins. I should know; tonight and tomorrow I'll be one of them."

JUDY had a mental picture of Tim as half-drowned by the time she crawled into bed Saturday night, but he showed up the next afternoon in plenty of time to drive her to Sandys Winter's for supper, even if he did look tireder than she had ever seen him.

"I nearly brought you an aqualung," she told him sympathetically. "Wasn't it pretty ghastly?"

"If you'd trotted over with a couple of hot bricks for our feet, we'd have fallen on your neck," he admitted. "I had on three pairs of woolen socks under my boots, but my toes aren't thawed out yet. After this weekend that bird had better hire himself an army for a body-guard. If the rangers ever lay hands on him, he'll need one to keep us from stringing him up on that gallows outside the Station."

"And, of course, he didn't show," Judy said with resignation.

Tim snorted. "Nothing showed except water, but

134

there was enough of that to make up for any other lacks. For Pete's sake, though, Judy, help me cover if I slip and say anything I shouldn't tonight. Mr. Winter's overboard now worrying about the trouble this business has caused everybody else. He'd have a fit if he knew we'd been patrolling."

Fortunately, a supper cooked by Elvira Snow and served by candlelight in front of a blazing fire was calculated to make anyone forget rain sluicing down his dining-room windows, and between them, Judy and Tim maneuvered the conversation safely around to the history of the old house and Sinnett Harbor.

"Firelight, marvelous food, and good stories," Judy said finally. "What more could we want?"

They had taken their coffee into the living room with them, and she was almost sorry when she saw Mr. Winter look at the clock and then reach for the phone. There were fatigue lines around his eyes that troubled her. Still, it might help to have even this one question settled, and the sooner he got his call through, the sooner she and Tim could leave and let him rest.

The minutes kept ticking off, however, and the call was still not completed. "I'll fight it out on this line if it takes all summer," Mr. Winter quoted disgustedly after the operator had reported for the third time that there was no answer. "I'm getting stubborn about it. Let's go over the whole story from beginning to end while we wait. Maybe one of us will have a brain storm."

No brain storms had materialized, though, when the phone rang again at ten o'clock and the operator made her final report.  She had got through to Mr. John Allison's New York apartment, but Mr. Allison's return had been delayed by storm conditions in the south.  He was not expected now before nine the next evening.  Should she try again then?  Mr. Winter's "yes" was emphatic, but the three of them stared at each other, feeling deflated.

"Well, while there's life, there's hope," Tim said feebly, and their host summoned up the ghost of a smile.

"It isn't much of a hope at best, I'm afraid," he said. "Still, you never know.  I'll give each of you a ring as soon as I do reach Jack Allison."

In spite of himself, there was an exhausted note in Sandys Winter's voice, and Judy exchanged a worried glance with Tim as they rose to go.  There was no one who considered himself less and other people more, and even thinking of that twisted shadowy figure skulking around the Ridge made her boil.

"I'm planning to sit by the phone all tomorrow evening, worrying my head off about fitting John Paul Jones' sword into Bold Dick's cupboard," she announced so firmly that both men began to chuckle. "After all, we've checked and double-checked and eliminated every other possibility tonight.  You know the theory that Mr. Teed's detective works on: if you eliminate the possible, the improbable is the answer, and he never makes a mistake!"

A tattoo from a banging shutter drummed Judy's eyes open early Monday morning, and she made a dive for her window.  The rain now was driving in wind-blown gusts that threatened to saturate the foot of her bed. This was the worst yet. At least they had not had a gale to worry about over the weekend. Down below she could see Captain Matt determinedly closing the first-floor shutters, and she noted with dismay how much strength he had to exert to budge them against the force of the wind. The weather news must be pretty grim, she thought, and her mind flew back to Mr. Winter. His house on Gibbet Ridge was even more exposed than the houses here on the Foreside. If he had to batten down, too, she only hoped the rangers got there before he tried to do the job himself.

Shivering into knee-high socks and wool Bermudas, Judy listened to the faint sounds of an announcer's voice drifting up the stairs. Mrs. Matt was apparently glued to the weather report, but for the moment that one look out the window had told Judy more than enough. Unless she craved to spend the day waterlogged, she would have to carry her skirt along in her rain pouch. Not even her boots and slicker would keep the lower half of her dry today. There was one consolation, though. She certainly would not be taking the bookmobile out, and she could stay put once she reached the library. She would rather skip lunch than struggle across Ship Street.

But there was a box of sandwiches and a quart thermos of coffee waiting for her on the dining-room table when she hurried down to join the Dunnings for breakfast.

"It wasn't a mite of trouble," Mrs. Matt said, waving

away thanks. "There's no sense tramping out to a drugstore on a day like this, Judy. Look at that slicker of Matt's dripping a lake on the floor! And it's bound to get worse before it gets better. Hurricane Carol struck the Carolinas and Virginia last night. They're in a state of disaster."

"Oh, how ghastly," Judy exclaimed in horror. "No wonder we've picked up a wind. I hope she had the decency to blow herself out."

"Not yet," Captain Matt said grimly. "There's no telling whether she'll head out to sea or not, but whatever she does, the whole coast is in for a full gale. Wind's clocking now at sixty miles an hour here, and with an incoming tide that's more than enough."

Finishing his last cup of coffee, he strode over to the closet and dug out his hip boots. "Figure I'd better lash down movable gear aboard the schooners and the clipper while I can get out to them comfortably," he explained. "Long about noon it's liable to turn ornery. Weight of this wind's going to give us a storm tide that'll seem like flood a couple of hours early."

"You'd better stop aboard the *Triton,* too, Matt, before Sand Winter tries to kill himself battening down alone," his wife told him, worried.

Captain Matt nodded. "I'm aiming to," he said briefly. "Skin into your slicker, Judy, and I'll drop you at the library on my way."

Even with a lift, though, Judy felt as if she needed to stop and shake herself like a St. Bernard by the time she reached the staff room. If this was Captain Matt's idea of comfortable weather for rowing out to the *Ellen,* he could have it. She had never seen Ship Street look more deserted. The only stores doing any business were the food markets. The rest of the Harbor merchants were obviously in for a dull day. For that matter, she realized with satisfaction, so was the library. Maybe this was the day the staff had been praying for all summer when they'd catch up with themselves just for once.

Buttoning her skirt hastily over her shorts, Judy headed for her desk and started on the stack of "over-due" notices she had been trying to address for the last three days. But Miss Leonard gave her staff small chance to catch up on anything. She had moved the staff-room radio onto her own desk, and with WGAN in Portland croaking warnings like Cassandra, she was far more concerned with the present situation than she was with the piled-up detail jobs from past weeks. The panes in all the windows on the southeast side of the building were bowing perceptibly inward, and if they gave way, every book in the stacks below them would be ruined.

"Somehow we've got to get those shutters closed," she told the rest of them. "Of course, it's Charley Hodgekin's job, but one of the joys of sharing a janitor on this Mall is that he's always just left for some other building when any of us needs him!"

Beside her, the radio crackled into speech again, and they listened, aghast. Hurricane Carol had raked Long Island, leaving a trail of death and destruction in her wake. National Guard units and Civil Defense personnel were already in action, and the Red Cross was mobilized.

"Stand by for emergency reports," Portland warned. "There is still hope for the New England coast; Carol may turn inland, blowing out over Vermont and New Hampshire without major damage, but all New England is alerted. We repeat: stand by for emergency reports."

"The suggestion seems superfluous," Miss Leonard said drily. "If there's anyone who isn't listening now, it's because he's deaf. Mercy on us, hear that wind. It's still rising. We'd better hurry with those shutters."

"We ought to be able to close them if we use a stepladder," Judy said. She slid out of her skirt again and grinned at their page. "How about it, Pat? You're in dungarees."

"Sure we can close 'em," Pat agreed cheerfully. "We're rugged."

But they were not rugged enough to suit Miss Leonard. After she had opened the side screen door and had it yanked off its upper hinges before she could pull it closed again, she flatly refused to let either of them stand on top of a ladder outside. "We'll have to hook them with that crook-handled cane somebody left here the other day," she insisted, and Judy promptly straddled a sill. It took them nearly an hour, though, to close the first three, and only what Pat called "Yankee cussedness" made them tackle the last one at all.

"I feel like a lady wrestler," Judy admitted when she finally climbed down. "I'll probably have Charley horse for a week."

"I'm more afraid you'll both have pneumonia," Miss Leonard said, looking worried. "Your hair couldn't be wetter if you'd stood on your heads in pails of water, and I don't dare build a fire in the browsing room. There's too much suction in the chimney. Blazing chunks sailing out over the roof would be the last straw."

She hunted up towels and ordered them to rub their heads while she and Miss Addison fixed a couple of cans of soup. "It's only eleven-thirty, but it won't hurt any of us to stop and eat. At least, the weather report is still encouraging. That ought to help our digestion."

Hot soup to go with Mrs. Matt's sandwiches and coffee warmed even Pat and Judy eventually, and in spite of the menacing roar of the wind around the building, they all felt a lessening of tension.

"Perhaps I'll get some cataloguing done after all," Miss Addison began optimistically. "If Carol—" She broke off hastily and sat listening in silence. The siren atop the town hall across the Mall was screaming urgent warning.

"Oh, no," Judy gasped. "Not fire in this gale!"

But Pat was already shaking her head, her happy-go-lucky young face sober as their ears caught the fainter wails of the auxiliary sirens drifting downwind from Gun Point and the Foreside.

"I have to go, Miss Leonard," she said, streaking out of the room, and Judy stared after her with a sick feeling in the pit of her stomach. Pat was a member of the high-school emergency shore patrol.

"That means a boat's in trouble, doesn't it?" she asked miserably.

Miss Leonard nodded, but the phone on the circulation desk began to ring imperiously and she hurried over to answer it. "By all means use mine," she said after a moment. "There's a set of keys under the right front fender in one of those magnetic holders." Then she set the receiver back, her expression grave. "It must be worse outside than we guessed," she told the other two. "That was Dr. Elliott needing my car. An elm's toppled and crushed his. It's a breeches-buoy job down at the shore. A summer cruise windjammer with thirty aboard is dismasted off Bushy Head. Both Dr. Elliott and Dr. Holliday have been called. At least half a dozen are injured." She turned her head sharply toward the radio on her own desk. "Listen, there comes WGAN again. Try changing the volume control, will you, please, Judy. The static's terrific."

Before Judy could move, however, the announcer's voice filled the room. "Emergency coastal warning! Hurricane Carol has struck Connecticut and Cape Cod and is heading for Rhode Island at an accelerated speed. The eye will pass through Portland at approximately 2:30 P.M. on a northeasterly course. Emergency coastal warning! There is no hope of Carol's turning inland. The eye will pass through Portland at approximately 2:30 P.M. with winds up to 135 miles an hour. Stand by for further reports."

For a second the three in the library stared around them blankly. Then Miss Leonard roused herself for action. "We'll be about thirty minutes behind Port-land getting the brunt of it," she calculated swiftly. "With no car, we must be out of here by two-fifteen—which gives us a little over an hour to do what we can. Check all the windows first, please, Miss Addison, and pull the switches in the wing. The place will be safer with the current off. Judy, come help me get those canvases the painters left down in the basement. If the shingles go, this floor will be drenched. We've got to cover what we can."

After that, the three of them worked silently and methodically, dragging the canvases up the stairs and hauling them over the tops of stacks. And when the canvases gave out, they used the linoleum rugs from the staff room and the children's room. Climbing up and down a ladder, tugging and pulling, Judy felt the muscles of her arms shrieking protest, but there was no time to stop and rest. Their hour had run out and Miss Leonard was hurrying them into their slickers.

"We've done all we can," she said wearily as they struggled out the front door into the storm. "The rest of the place will have to take its chances. Be sure to give the door an extra slam, will you, Judy. Sometimes it doesn't quite catch."

But Judy was gesturing back over her shoulder at the reading room. "We forgot to put out the light on the circulation desk," she shouted over the wind. "You two go on. I'll turn it off and fasten the door, Miss Leonard."

## 17 · Emergency Call

**D**ASHING across the lobby into the reading room, Judy groped hurriedly for the baseplug under the circulation desk and disconnected the lamp. If what she had encountered outside was only the preliminary blow, she had no desire to loiter and be caught in anything worse, not when she had to fight in the teeth of the wind all the way back to the Foreside. But before she had got more than halfway to the door again, the telephone shrilled after her. "Oh, drat!" she muttered and tore back. Now that Miss Leonard had left, it was probably Dr. Elliott saying he had brought her car over.

It was not Dr. Elliott on the line, however. In fact, it did not seem to be anybody. All she could hear was a weird panting sound. Apparently something had gone wrong with the connection, and she frowned impatiently. "Sinnett Harbor Public Library," she repeated. "Can you hear me?"

"Judy?" The voice at the other end was a whispered

gasp, and Judy's knuckles whitened on the receiver. That queer, strangled whisper could not be the fault of the connection. Something was dreadfully wrong.

"Yes, it's Judy," she said, frightened. "Oh, what's the matter? Who is it, please?"

For a moment she thought there was going to be no answer. Then the painful voice labored on.

"Sandys—Winter," it panted. "Sorry—to—trouble —you. Send—Dr.—Elliott—if—you—"

The voice at the other end faded out, and Judy's heart lurched.

"Mr. Winter! Mr. Winter!" she called, frantic. But there was no answering whisper, and she buried her face in her hands, trying to force herself to think calmly. She couldn't send Dr. Elliott, or old Dr. Holliday either. She couldn't even reach them. And there weren't any other doctors. But Mr. Winter was having a heart attack! She'd have to rouse the rangers. At least they had an oxygen tank.

Grabbing the receiver off its cradle, she did not even wait for service. "Operator! Operator!" she called. "The Ranger Station! Emergency!" What an idiot she was anyway. Jimmy's father was right there in the Park. Tim would get Dr. Merrill. Still the operator failed to answer, and Judy jiggled the switch bar indignantly. There could not be anything wrong with the line. She had just stopped talking to Mr. Winter. But suddenly panic choked her and she looked hopelessly up at the ceiling. The overhead light she had switched on was flickering out. The power lines were down. And in the slow motion of despair Judy set the receiver methodically back in place. She could not phone anybody. Then almost without conscious volition she was across the room and stumbling down the stairs behind the stacks. The basement door would be closest to the garage. There was no other way to reach Dr. Merrill. She would have to take the bookmobile.

The shock of icy wind and rain in her face jerked Judy out of her numbed daze, and she headed the station wagon down the driveway, her mind racing with the wheels. The full force of the hurricane would not strike for half an hour and she could put a lot of miles behind her in thirty minutes! But once out on Ship Street, Judy knew better. The road was already littered with a tangled mass of trees and wires that she'd have to jockey the bookmobile around. She could not even afford to take chances. If she piled up, it might be night before anyone else happened on Mr. Winter. Only she could not understand it. Why was he alone? Where under the sun was Elvira?

Beneath her hands, with the pull of the wind, the steering wheel kept jumping like a live thing, and her grip tightened. Only three more miles to Gallows Road, she reminded herself doggedly. But driving them turned into a nightmare of inching the bookmobile under trees tilted crazily over the highway and jamming the accelerator desperately to the floor to shoot by tottering utility poles. Hanging grimly to the wheel, the shriek of the storm a throbbing ache in her ears, Judy began to think the miles were endless. Then all at once wind-tortured elms were looming up just ahead, marking the crossroads, and she stepped hard on the gas again with a reckless feeling of triumph. She had reached Gallows Road! Somehow she would make it the rest of the way.

But over the flooded marshes along the inlet the wind roared in like a mad demon, snatching at the bookmobile, shaking it, flinging salt-laden spray across the windshield, and Judy's surge of triumph vanished. Somewhere back in the nightmare of Ship Street the rain had stopped, but this was worse. Visibility was bad now, and a salt crust could stop her. Driving with her head out the window would be impossible. In the face of that wind she would not be able to keep her eyes open. Stubbornly Judy fought the station wagon into the right-hand lane and set her windshield wipers in motion. She had only two choices: give up or speed up, and deliberately she rocketed the station wagon forward. If she couldn't give up, she had to take a calculated risk. I only have to use my head and keep my eyes open, she told herself firmly. Like Tim when he didn't know what kind of snake he'd find in the bananas. After all, in a southeast gale Gallows Road had to be clear; it just made sense. There was nothing that could blow across it except salt water. Even the telephone poles were on the west side and they were crashing on top of the splintered pines in Gun Point Park. She could slow down for the wooded stretch just this side of the Park gateposts where the road curved away from the inlet and followed the outside shore.

147

Fantastically, though, it was not uprooted pines that made Judy slam on her brakes at the curve, and she stared from the snarling water of Pentecost Bay back to the lobster boat flung across the road in front of her wheels as if she did not quite believe in either of them. "Now I've seen everything," she gasped. The bookmobile could no more squeeze past that battered wreck than it could have squeezed past the Empire State Building dropped down in its path. She backed hastily into the shelter of a retaining wall a dozen yards down the road before she climbed out. At least it could not possibly take long to make the Ranger Station now. The Park entrance was almost in sight.

Arguing on foot with a hurricane, however, was time-consuming, and it took fifteen hectic minutes of battling to get back to the lobster boat and struggle over it. Somehow she had to make better time! But the road ahead was an impassable shambles of tree trunks and bushes and wire fencing. Judy could feel herself getting panicky again, and if she really clutched, she thought disgustedly, she was finished. To get into the Park at all now she needed her wits in working order, not in a tailspin. Around her, trees were toppling like pins in a bowling alley, and her heart contracted at the devastation. It had taken forever to grow those magnificent old giants, but across the road above the rocky ledges there was not even one left standing.

Her gaze still riveted on the fallen pines, Judy's eyes narrowed speculatively. The ledges! Why hadn't she thought of them sooner! All she had to do was crawl, and dropping on her knees, she inched around the piles of debris onto the rocks. After that, with the wind clawing at her, Judy was too busy fighting for breath to worry about time. She only knew that from the way her knees felt she was crawling from here to eternity. Then, amazingly, her hands clutched at a gatepost, and she was on her feet again plunging through tangles of broken bayberry into the Park. Even through the flying spray, she could make out a ranger in a storm jacket doing something to the screen door at the Station, and she practically catapulted herself across the road to the steps. There was no use shouting. The wind would swallow her voice. Anyway it didn't matter! It was Tim up there on the porch and he was already turning around. Only what on earth was wrong with him? He looked as if he had seen a ghost.

Tim's face was white when he pulled Judy up beside him and he sounded furious enough to tar and feather Miss Leonard.

"Is she crazy?" he stormed. "You might have been killed! She had no business sending the bookmobile out."

"But Miss Leonard didn't send me," Judy panted. "She doesn't even know I took the bookmobile." She shook his arm frantically. "Tim, please stop ranting and listen. It's Mr. Winter! He had a heart attack, and I couldn't get Dr. Elliott. Everybody's over on Bushy Head. A boat's in trouble. Then the wires went down and there wasn't any other way to reach you. You've got to get Dr. Merrill, Tim. And hurry!

It's taken me forever to get here and Mr. Winter's alone. Something must have happened to Elvira."

"Her sister's sick," Tim explained hastily. "She left for Yarmouth early this morning." He was already yanking open the steel lockers on the porch and thrusting a storm lantern at Judy. "You'll need it," he told her. "I closed all the shutters on the Ridge after breakfast and it's getting darker by the minute. And for Pete's sake, don't trip over that cage!"

Grabbing the oxygen tank, he steered her safely past the pine snake's box, and hurried her across the road. But even while she ran, Judy was shaking his arm violently again.

"Tim," she gasped. "That cage was open. Where's Junior?"

"On the prowl, I guess," Tim admitted. "I never got a chance to put his cage inside and the wind tore the lid loose just before you got here. It's nothing to get into a flap about, Judy. If he doesn't like the weather, he'll hole up somewhere. He's safe as a church."

"Safe!" Judy repeated in consternation. "If you think I'm worrying about Junior! Suppose he tries his holing up in somebody's cabin. Another heart attack is all we need!"

## 18 · Mask Off

TIM refused to be stampeded by Judy's picture of the potential hazards in his pine snake's freedom. "Relax," he said patiently. "He won't crawl any couple of miles to a cabin in this weather."

"Maybe not," Judy conceded. "Only if he does, I hope to goodness he picks on Jimmy Merrill's!"

Actually she was too tired to have enough energy left to worry about anything except Mr. Winter. The peak of the hurricane was over, but the going was as bad as ever, and she plowed after Tim feeling as though this was exactly where she had come in. The same staggering gusts of wind still mauled her shoulders and the same clutter of fallen trees had to be climbed.

"What I've needed most all afternoon is a prehensile tail," she told Tim with a feeble grin when he hauled her by main force out of a shattered pine in front of the house on the Ridge. "I've been roosting in branches so long I feel like a monkey anyway, but give me credit for not getting stuck until you were handy!"

"You'd have come unstuck all right," Tim said with conviction. "I'll never figure out how you got here at all." Handing over the oxygen tank, he dug hastily down in his pocket for a package of matches and tilted her face up to his. "Don't lug that tank a step farther than you have to, and light your lantern as soon as you get inside," he ordered firmly. "You'll break your neck if you don't, Judy. Bold Dick made those shutters so thick they'd stop a British bullet and they still haven't got even a wormhole in 'em. The place is a morgue when they're closed."

Then unexpectedly he bent his head and kissed her hard. "I hate to leave you to go in alone," he said vehemently, and watching him vanish behind the debris on the road, Judy ran for the door with her shoulders squared again. "I feel almost as important as snakes," she thought dreamily. "We should have had a hurricane sooner."

For once she was even ready to bless Sinnett Harbor's antiquated door fastenings. With both hands full, lifting a wrought-iron latch was a whole lot easier than coping with a key and a doorknob, and she was grateful to get inside without having to park the oxygen tank in the pools of water on the porch. Unfortunately, though, nothing she could do would make the door stay closed after her. The latch seemed hopelessly sprung, and she gave up in frustrated exasperation. After all, what major harm can it do? she thought impatiently. The house faced west, away from the storm wind, and she certainly could not shoot the bolt on the inside when Tim and Dr. Merrill had to get in.

Just the same, the combination of half-open door and salt-laden spray outside did nothing to make the hall less bleak, and Judy shivered a little when she turned away. Tim was right. But the house was like a morgue in more ways than one. The silence was so thick she could hear her thoughts rattle, and she ran across to the living room with her lantern, feeling too much like Lady Macbeth in the sleepwalking scene for comfort. Only there was no sense going in there first, she decided hastily. If Mr. Winter was as sick as he sounded, he was probably still on the studio couch in the library beside his phone, and she hurried on to the next doorway, her hands suddenly clammy. It had taken her so long to get here! Anything might have happened. But nothing her imagination conjured up had prepared Judy for Sandys Winter's crumpled, unconscious figure, his hands and feet bound with his own kitchen towels, and she flung herself across the room shaking with frightened anger. Alone and sick—and this time the thief hadn't waited till midnight!

Snatching at the afghan on the foot of the couch, she threw it over Mr. Winter's shoulders and began to work feverishly on the knots in the binding around his ankles. If only Tim and Dr. Merrill would come, she thought despairingly. She needed a fire in the fireplace and blankets from upstairs, but these towels were not helping Mr. Winter's circulation. His legs were like chunks of ice. She dared not stop now to take care of the other jobs herself. Then miraculously she heard footsteps in the passage to the living room behind her, and she lifted her head a second with a strangled sob of relief. Somehow the road along the shore must have been open enough to let Dr. Merrill's car through!

"In the library, Tim. Hurry," she called urgently.

Strangely, though, she got no reassuring hail from Tim, and she started to turn, half rising from her knees in bewilderment, when a cold voice flicked at her like a whiplash. "Don't move! Stay where you are," it ordered, and she shrank down again, rigid, beside Mr. Winter, her eyes staring in fascinated horror at the twisted shadow moving across the path of her lantern light on the wall. I should have had brains enough to look, she thought numbly. But the cold voice was beating at the back of her head again, and she knelt there, forcing herself to listen. She couldn't go to pieces now!

"Where did Winter put the package you brought?" it demanded. "Don't bother to say you don't know. I was watching when you pulled the shades down for him."

Biting her lips, Judy kept her eyes glued to the reflection on the wall and shook her head in silence. If she did not speak, that voice would go on, and suddenly that was all she wanted. Its harsh, flat monotone was as unnatural as the misshapen shadow in front of her —like a weird distortion of something familiar, and caution gone, she flung her head up, waiting.

"I told you not to move, Miss Carrington!" the harsh

154

voice rasped. "And start talking. You're wasting my time."

There was an ugly edge to the cold monotone now, but Judy was no longer even listening. That "Miss Carrington" had been what she needed, and in a revulsion of contempt she twisted defiantly around.

"You!" she choked, but her scorn filled the quiet room as though she had shouted. "No wonder you hide behind a mask! A sick, old man alone in a house. Why you coward!"

Hot with anger, she had forgotten danger existed, but without warning his hand shot out, striking at her shoulder, and she slid sidewise, trying to crawl out of his reach. Then, panic-stricken, she saw him snatch the poker from the fireplace and she clutched desperately at the handle of the storm lantern.

"Don't come near me!" she panted. "This thing is hot enough to raise blisters."

With a yell of terror, however, he was already backing away from her, flailing the poker like a madman, and in dazed, incredulous wonder, Judy heard her own voice screaming encouragement at six feet of rattling, hissing fury on the fiber rug.

"Get him, Junior. Good snake! Get him."

Too late to dodge, though, she saw the poker slashing toward her head, and suddenly the floor rose up to meet her.

"Judy!"

Vaguely, a long way off, Judy could hear somebody calling her persistently, and she stirred a little, bothered. Her head ached and the voice was a million miles away. It wasn't worth the trouble of answering. Only now raindrops were trickling off her nose, and she finally dragged her eyelids open.

"Judy!"

"Yes?" she said politely. But for some reason it was hard to focus on the face bending over her. It was much easier just to lie there, letting her thoughts wander, aimless. Water was trickling off her nose again, though, and her eyes hurried back to the head above her. Why, it was Tim calling her. Only his voice was terribly husky. No wonder she hadn't known it. He must have a sore throat. For a minute she stared up puzzled. That hadn't been rain she felt either. She was inside a house. But why was Tim splashing water on her face and why was she lying on the floor? Then memory began to flood back, and she struggled frantically to sit up.

"Mr. Winter!" she gasped. "Glen Teed tied him with towels. Tim, don't let him get away. He's the Shadow!"

Before Tim could stop her, she was on her feet, swaying dizzily, and he snatched her hastily up in his arms.

"Everything's under control, Judy," he assured her, but his voice was still husky as he looked down at her white face. "Teed's hog-tied in the next room with a couple of rangers standing over him. He ran smack into the Chief's arms trying to back away from my pine snake. And if you look over my shoulder you can see Dr. Merrill's taking care of Mr. Winter. He's even sent the Chief across to the Harbor with the Coast Guard hunting for Dr. Elliott. They'll find him all right. The Coast Guard said everybody got rescued from that windjammer before their boat reached here."

Holding on to her as though he never again expected to trust her out of his reach, Tim turned around and started purposefully for the couch under the library windows. "I'm through letting you take chances," he warned her with a lopsided smile. "You're going to stay put and covered up till Dr. Merrill has a chance to look at your head if I have to sit on you!"

But Judy was not paying much attention to his orders. It was taking all the energy she could muster to look around the room over his shoulder.

"Junior," she said suddenly. "He's gone, Tim. Put me down quick. Mr. Teed was slashing at him with the poker. We've got to find him. Maybe he's hurt."

Tim, however, promptly tightened his arms around her. "Junior can darn well take care of himself," he said with great distinctness, but his voice grew husky again when her battered head slipped down on his shoulder. "Judy, you darling idiot, how can I stop to worry about a snake when there's you?"

## 19 · Mission Accomplished

DID you say 'darling?' " Judy asked as Tim parked her on the couch and dropped down on his knees beside her.

"I'll say I did," he said emphatically, "and I'm likely to say it again if you look at me that way." Stripping off his jacket, he wrapped it around her shoulders, kissing her thoroughly in the process. "Judy, how on earth could I hang around all summer without falling in love with you?" he demanded.

He bent over with every intention of kissing her again, and Judy stared up at him, her eyes suddenly dreamy. "I knew we should have had a hurricane sooner," she said contentedly. "Only, my goodness, how are you going to break it to Junior? He still isn't sure he likes me!"

She sounded so normal that Tim chuckled with relief. "We'll use bribery," he told her, grinning. "Junior's getting lazy. Having dinner handed out is a lot easier than bothering to catch his own mice. He'll show when he gets hungry and you can feed him a dozen eggs. You can bet your bottom dollar he kept safely out of the way of that poker." He smiled down at her again, but his lips set in a tight line as he made another hasty examination of the discolored lump on the top of her head. "It's a good thing for Teed somebody else is guarding him," he admitted grimly. "I'd have a tough time keeping my hands off his neck!"

"I don't have to see him again now, do I, Tim?" Judy asked, shivering, and he shook his head.

"I can't see why you have to look at him until some judge is ready to throw the book at him, Judy. The Chief's bringing Captain Matt back with him, and the two of them'll take care of Teed. They'll probably turn him over to the state troopers later. But what I want to know is how he got wind of that package. You hadn't even dug it out of the bookmobile when he drove off Friday."

"He didn't drive very far," Judy said, and anger brought a little color back to her white face. "He just parked and sneaked up under a window. He told me he watched us till we pulled the shades. That's why he was sure I knew where the package was. You see, I was pretty dumb, Tim. I thought it was you and Dr. Merrill coming when I was untying Mr. Winter and I yelled for you to hurry. Then suddenly there was that twisted shadow on the wall in front of me."

Watching the color drain from her face, Tim's fists clenched angrily. "For my money, the guy's sub-human," he growled. "Anyway, he's sure washed up now. Between breaking and entering and atrocious assault, he's for it."

"But I don't think he meant to hit me," Judy said slowly. "At least not with the poker. He was so scared of Junior he just flailed around and my head was in his way." She raised herself gingerly on one elbow and turned a worried face toward the studio couch. "It's what he did to Mr. Winter that's so awful. Please go and ask Dr. Merrill if we can help him, Tim. There's nothing the matter with me except a headache. Honestly."

Tim, however, still vetoed the idea of her moving. "Any running around that's done I do," he announced with such firmness that she finally settled back. But he kept a stern eye on her until the Chief's hastily recruited relief squad arrived and he could carry her upstairs at Dr. Merrill's orders, with Mrs. Matt on his heels to put her to bed. "Everything's going to be okay," he reassured her as she meekly swallowed some sleeping pills. "That nurse the Coast Guard brought over even says Dr. Elliott thinks Mr. Winter will be all right. I'll tear in at dawn with all the news."

It was afternoon, though, before Tim or anybody else got another glimpse of Judy. He had shown up looking hopeful about breakfast time, but Mrs. Matt had shooed him unceremoniously, and Captain Matt and the Chief Ranger got the same treatment at eleven.

"She's got a mild concussion and the doctor said she was to sleep till she waked of her own accord," she told them all with finality. "My land, with you men pant-

160

ing like bloodhounds, it's a good thing there's a doctor and a nurse in the house to keep you on leash!"

But when Mrs. Matt did let them see Judy, she was propped against her pillows with an ice bag perched rakishly on her head, thoroughly wide-awake and thoroughly disgusted for fear she had missed something.

"Hurry up and tell me everything," she begged the minute the three of them appeared in the door, and Captain Matt's eyes twinkled.

"Sounds practically as good as new," he told the other two happily, patting her hand. "But we're going to catch Hail Columbia from Jen if we stay too long. We haven't got much news anyway, Judy. We still don't know what Teed was after. The Chief just wants to ask you a question."

The Chief Ranger nodded. "We need your help again, Miss Carrington," he said briskly. "Teed isn't volunteering a thing, but he claims he merely followed you in here yesterday, planning to get some information out of you. He insists he knows nothing of the attack on Sandys Winter."

For a second Judy looked from one to the other of them, speechless. Then she sat bolt upright, clutching at her ice bag and sputtering. "I suppose he was just out for a stroll in the hurricane with a stocking mask pulled over his head," she exclaimed. "That's a hot one when he'd already told me he hated to set foot outside in bad weather!"

Tim grinned at her sympathetically and the Chief nodded again. "That's the general idea," he said drily.

161

"The yarn raised Captain Matt's blood pressure, too."
Reaching into his pocket, he pulled out a key and
dropped it on her palm. "Take a look at it for us, will
you, Miss Carrington? It fell out of Winter's trouser
cuff when we carried him upstairs last night. Is it
yours, by any chance?"

Judy shook her head. "I only had the set for the
station wagon with me," she said. But turning it over,
curious, she gave an excited gasp. "Why, it belongs to
one of the filing cabinets in a workshop at the library.
Look," she pointed at the figures stamped in the metal.
"I made a list of those serial numbers for Miss Leonard
and they're easy to remember. They begin at 149020
and this is 149026. Now let Mr. Teed try to prove he
came in after I did! He's had that key all summer,
Chief."

She leaned back against her pillows triumphantly as
the Chief Ranger stowed the key away in his wallet.
"You've handed it to us on a platter," he told her with
grim satisfaction. "Teed'll make it as tough as he can.
It's easy to trip a psychopathic liar, but this man only
lies when he has a chance to get away with it. He was
careful to keep out of sight until after you found Winter. He knew you couldn't prove a thing, and that attack's the most serious charge he faces. After all, what
else have we got against him—that he broke into four
places and didn't take even a pin!"

Seeing Captain Matt tap his watch significantly, the
Chief rose hastily to his feet. "We'll keep you in
touch," he assured Judy. "We can't wire Allison in

162

New York, worse luck, not until service is restored, but I'm still hoping Teed will crack when he finds out he stuck his neck in a noose for nothing. Wade says that package just had a manuscript in it."

"A first novel by an unknown author at that," Judy agreed. "Mr. Teed could have stayed safely holed up in his cabin." But she had hardly finished the sentence before she gave a strangled cry and began pointing wildly. "Tim!" she gasped. "Mr. Teed! The window."

Tim's fist banged disgustedly on the back of a chair. "Oh, for Pete's sake, how dumb can we get?" he demanded. "You don't need to wire Mr. Allison, Chief. Teed told Judy he was watching us through the window Friday. He knew what was in that package. He saw Mr. Winter open it. Don't ask us why, but he wanted that manuscript. Now maybe he'll tell us what this is all about!"

## 20 · *Moonlight and Junior*

CTUALLY, it was the end of the week before the whole sorry story was clear. Tim had had trouble opening Bold Dick's secret cupboard, but once confronted with the manuscript, Glen Teed broke down. Jerry Ricker had left the revised copy of his mystery with the older man's name and address clipped to it, and the landlady had dutifully shipped it on, explaining that it was the only piece of writing the young man had left. One reading had been enough for Teed. His last two books had failed to win the smashing success of his *Midnight Means Murder,* and this manuscript had everything. Consequently, when he learned by accident from Sandys Winter in New York that some other copy was in existence and on its way to him, Teed had taken the first train to Sinnett Harbor to intercept the package. It was the only way he could prevent exposure. He had appropriated the manuscript. That was his new book, scheduled for early publication and already sold to the movies.

Tim had been right in thinking Teed believed the house on the Ridge empty that first night. He had gone there directly from his train, assuming Sandys Winter was still in New York, but he was too well known from his summers in Sinnett Harbor not to take precautions. Making use of his theatrical training, he had twisted himself up, lopping inches off his six feet three, and added the mask for good measure. The rest of the story they all knew. He had had to be cautious after he was spotted on the Ridge, but by moving into a Park cabin he had been in a position to work fast if the manuscript arrived at the Winter house, and by using a library workshop, he could watch for any express packages delivered to Sandys Winter's office. He had investigated the first one that arrived, bursting it open apparently by accident when he helped Judy set up the Bold Dick Week exhibits, but after that, he had to resort to breaking into the library at night and to trailing Captain Matt. He had already planned the library entry when he refused to share his cabin on the opening night of *The Lady and the Pirate;* he wanted no witnesses to the time of his return. Meanwhile, he had kept in close contact with Sandys Winter and, during his absence, with Judy. They were his best sources of information.

"Stealing a dead man's manuscript and palming it off as your own is about the lowest thing I've struck yet," Judy said hotly Sunday night. She and Tim were eating supper beside a fire on Bold Dick Beach, but not even the orange moon rising over Pentecost Bay could keep her mind off Glen Teed. "What if his last book wasn't such a hit! Lots of times a man writes a best seller and then gets his next book really panned. Mr. Teed wasn't starving in a garret. He sold everything he wrote."

"The man's not quite human," Tim insisted. "He's got a mind like a calculating machine. Look at the way it worked in this business. Mr. Winter gets a copy of that manuscript and wants to have it published because the author's mother needs the money. Teed gets hold of one and figures it's so much gravy. If murder would have got him out of the mess he'd made for himself, he'd probably have murdered that landlady without any compunctions. It's sure going to kill him to cough up that ten thousand Hollywood paid him! But he played into luck again on one thing, Judy. He'd be really up against it if Mr. Winter weren't going to get well."

"But it's no thanks to him," Judy said indignantly. "As if a heart attack weren't enough in the first place! And every time I remember us thanking him over at the library for bringing in our packages for us, I burn up. Only I still don't see why he waited till the middle of the hurricane to hunt for that manuscript when he saw us give it to Mr. Winter Friday."

"Because it was the first chance he got," Tim admitted. "Nobody was around then, but he'd caught us patrolling the Ridge last weekend. The weather was so foul we got careless I guess." Reaching over, he managed to pull Judy close enough to land a kiss on the end of her nose. "At least, Junior and I profited," he told her. "Junior approves of picnics, but it took Mr. Teed to get you to give him an invitation." Turning lazily, Tim took a look at the big snake busy swallowing eggs. "Talk about bribery and corruption," he said severely. "How many dozen of those things did you bring him? He's just getting around to the last one!"

There'd never be any changing Tim, Judy thought, watching his eyes linger on Junior. But she didn't want him changed. She grinned suddenly to herself, though, thinking of a soulful lady who had had her hunting all over the library yesterday for a Lovelace poem about loving honor more. "I could not love thee, dear, so much, loved I not *serpents* more," she misquoted wickedly.

Tim's arms promptly closed hard around her. "Take it back unless you want your ribs crushed being proved wrong," he ordered.

Behind them, Junior's last eggshell collapsed with a plop, and Judy smiled contentedly. "I can paddle a dugout bookmobile on the Amazon while you catch snakes. Don't ever change, Tim. I love you just exactly the way you are."

## About the Author

EDITH DORIAN knows a great deal about books and writing. Ever since her college days at Smith, she has been doing short stories, articles, and reviews, and for a number of years she taught literature at the New Jersey College for Women at Rutgers University. She has done special research at Harvard University and received her master's degree at Columbia University.

Each year Mrs. Dorian is in great demand for her book talks, and she is also very active in the civic affairs of New Brunswick, where the Dorians live. She is married to the Dean of Instruction at the New Jersey College for Women, and has two children.

Maine, the scene of THE TWISTED SHADOW, is a second home to Mrs. Dorian—her children are the fourth generation of her family to spend their summers there. And Mrs. Dorian knew Hurricane Carol only too well.

THE TWISTED SHADOW is her fifth junior book, her other four being NO MOON ON GRAVEYARD HEAD, HIGHWATER CARGO, TRAILS WEST AND MEN WHO MADE THEM (with W. N. Wilson)—all for teen-age readers—and ASK DR. CHRISTMAS, for readers in the middle group.

6310